The Hawthorn Tree & Other Stories by AM Burrage

Alfred McLelland Burrage was born in Hillingdon, Middlesex on 1st July, 1889. His father and uncle were both writers, primarily of boy's fiction, and by age 16 AM Burrage had joined them. The young man had ambitions to write for the adult market too. The money was better and so was his writing.

From 1890 to 1914, prior to the mainstream appeal of cinema and radio the printed word, mainly in magazines, was the foremost mass entertainment. AM Burrage quickly became a master of the market publishing his stories regularly across a number of publications.

By the start of the Great War Burrage was well established but in 1916 he was conscripted to fight on the Western Front. He continued to write during these years documenting his experiences in the classic book War is War by Ex-Private X.

For the remainder of his life Burrage was rarely printed in book form but continued to write and be published on a prodigious scale in magazines and newspapers. In this volume we concentrate on his supernatural stories which are, by common consent, some of the best ever written. Succinct yet full of character each reveals a twist and a flavour that is unsettling…..sometimes menacing….always disturbing.

There are many other volumes available in this series together with a number of audiobooks. All are available from iTunes, Amazon and other fine digital stores.

Table Of Contents

The Hawthorn Tree

They say that she died of a broken heart
I tell the tale as 'twas told to me

But her spirit lives, and her soul is part
Of this sad old house by the sea.
—Bret Harte

The road which takes one almost due west out of Hazelsea throws out a branch pointing straight to the north-west when, according to the finger post, one has walked or ridden a mile. At this road junction there is a triangular strip of turf, with a tall and aged hawthorn tree growing out of its centre. Close by, on the left-hand side of the left fork of the road, stands Maid's Rue, an Elizabethan cottage, which was—and probably still is—to be let furnished. Serringham took the place three years ago, after he had passed the first stages of a nervous breakdown.

Serringham had been told to go away to a quiet place and rest, and he could scarcely have found a quieter. Hazelsea is one of the dullest holes on the East Coast, and Maid's Rue was a mile removed from such dubious distractions as it was able to offer. Serringham preferred to go away alone, for most people worried him. 'But you don't count, old man,' he assured me.

'Come down and stay whenever you like.'

Serringham was engaged to my sister Pamela. He was a chartered accountant who had lately paid the penalty for months of over-work. He came and spent an evening with us after he had left the nursing-home. He was not his old self, but he seemed much more cheerful than I had expected, and he left London in quite an optimistic mood.

'I'm bound to like the cottage,' he assured us. I know it quite well from the outside. And a fellow I know who's been staying in Hazelsea has been over it for me, and says it's a perfect place inside. Been slightly modernised to make it habitable—bath-room, and all that, you know—but not in any way spoilt.'

So he went to Maid's Rue, and, as he had foretold, found himself completely satisfied. News of him, in the form of long letters, reached Pamela nearly every day and was retailed to me. The cottage was almost too good to be true, the strong air was doing him all the good in the world, he had found an excellent woman to come in and do the work, there were shelves laden with an excellent assortment of books—and when was I coming down to see him? I did not know if he really wanted me, but when at last he enclosed a note for me in one of his letters to Pamela, begging me to give him a weekend, I drove down.

There was no mistaking the cottage. Its locality was clearly defined by the cross-roads, and the gnarled and stunted old hawthorn tree which grew out of the triangular patch of turf. The red brick and timber cottage, which had an air of boasting its age and flaunting its decrepit beauties, stood close to the road. Its small and heavily-leaded windows were diamond-paned and its gabled roof was heavily thatched.

Inside it was necessarily dark. The rooms were low-pitched and the heavy beams a perpetual menace to a man of average height. The floors were of stone and the fireplace wide open, with those huge chimneys which must be specially beloved of Santa Claus. But I was not surprised at Serringham's enthusiasm for the place. In him was ingrained a love of old houses, and he was even able to make virtues of their inconveniences. I must own that the cottage was charmingly furnished. It was filled with genuine and solid old oak, and there were the inevitable grandfather clocks, warming-pans, turnspits, and chestnut roasters.

Serringham received me very cordially but very quietly. He raised his voice scarcely above a murmur, and presently explained that he had got into the way of speaking like that since coming to Maid's Rue.

'I'm a new man already,' he said. 'Don't you think I've improved?'

'Ye-es,' I answered, because I wasn't quite sure.

'Oh, I see.' He gave a slow and rather tired smile. 'You expected me to be boisterous, did you? Well, that's not a sign. The first thing a poor devil in my condition needs to achieve is peace of mind. That's coming back. It's splendid to wake in the morning and know that one has no work and no responsibilities. I've nothing to do but laze and slack about, and that's what suits me best just at present. I hope you won't want to get up too early, by the way?'

'If I do,' I promised him, i won't disturb you.'

'Oh, all right. Well, Mrs Hickory comes in every morning at eight, and you can have breakfast at half-past if you want it. You won't mind my not joining you, though. I spend a lot of time dreaming nowadays—day-dreaming you know. I suppose I always was a potential dreamer, and never before had the time to indulge myself.'

'Well, dream away, by all means, if it does you good!' I laughed.

'You've come to the right place for dreaming.'

'Yes, haven't I? It amuses me to sit here sometimes of a night and try to visualise the people who have lived here throughout the last four hundred years, all of whom have passed on and perhaps left behind them some impression of their personalities, if only we were attuned to picking them up. A house like this makes you think. I wonder how many lovers it has bred, and prodigal sons, and poor neglected wives, and knaves, and heroes, and happy hum-drum folk. These old walls must have seen strange sights and heard strange sounds. There's only one thing we can be sure about—that they've heard more weeping than laughter. That's the way of this beast of a world.'

'I wonder how the place got its name?' I remarked, it's a most curious one.'

Serringham's face brightened, and for the first time he raised his voice a little.

'Oh, I've found that out,' he said, i was going to tell you. It's a great story. One of the local traditions, you know. And I shouldn't be surprised if there's something in it. It seems that sometime over a hundred years ago—nobody can guess how long—there lived in this house a very beautiful girl who was notorious for her coquetries and her fickleness. She is supposed to have driven nearly all the young men in the neighbourhood to despair. And then, as so often happens in these cases, the biter was bitten. She gave her heart unreservedly to one man who made her drink the same bitter draught which she had given to so many.

'People die of broken hearts, you know, although not in the direct sense. Hers was broken, but it continued to beat, and so she stilled it forever by taking poison. And following the custom of the day, they buried her at the cross-roads with a stake driven through her heart. They buried her at the cross-roads outside, and the story is that the hawthorn tree which still grows there today sprang up from the green stake which transfixed her. Of course, I don't believe it, but it seems likely that somebody who loved her may have planted the tree with her body as a memorial to her.'

'It's poetical,' I said smiling, 'but I shouldn't think it's true. How long does a hawthorn live?'

'Don't ask me. But that must be a very old one. It's nearly dead now. Perhaps its death will be a sign that the poor girl whose dust helped to bring it life has worked her passage to some happy port. But isn't it a good story?'

'It's picturesque, certainly,' I agreed dryly. 'But it's a little morbid. Do you spend your time speculating on the lady?'

'It's only right and natural to give a thought or two to the next world sometimes. Yes, I catch myself wondering where she is, and if her spirit has spirit lovers. Perhaps sometimes she comes and peeps about these old rooms, and wonders why men don't see her, or why her charms, which only failed her once, no longer bring anybody to her feet. Oh, I know what's in your mind, my lad! You think it's wrong for a man in my condition to let his mind dwell on such things. You think I ought to go for long walks, and read Punch. But this contemplative sort of life happens to suit me, and whatever I like is surely best for myself.'

I doubted it, but I followed his line of reason. However, I changed the subject and began to tell him all about Pamela's recent doings. He listened politely enough, but now and then there came over his eyes something like a film, and it occurred to me that, for a fiance, he was not particularly interested in Pamela's doings. Before his illness he had been a very devoted lover. But he was a sick man still, and I had to remember it.

I rose early next morning and was downstairs before Mrs Hickory came. A strange sweet and sickly odour, faint and elusive, but still discernible, pervaded the house. I thought I recognised it; and I knew at the same time that I must be wrong. It was the smell of fresh may-blossom, and the month happened to be February.

It was a windy morning, cold but fine, with fleeting gleams of sunshine through gaps in a hurried procession of white clouds. I was in the mood for a walk before breakfast and let myself out. I crossed the road and passed over to the triangle of turf, from which the old hawthorn tree raised its slender gnarled trunk and bare, dark, tortured limbs.

The hedges around were already budding, but there was not the least pale pin-head of a leaf showing on the old tree. It looked to be going the way of all flesh, and all timber. Soon, I supposed, somebody would cut it down for firewood, and then nothing would be left in memory of the girl whose bones lay at its roots.

It was Sunday morning. Somewhere in the distance church bells were giving notice of an early service, and as I stood undecided which road to take, there came shambling towards me an old yokel in his Sunday clothes of rusty black, with shabby prayer-books in a great brown sinewy hand. He greeted me with a 'Fine marnin', sir,' and, seeing me to be a stranger, eyed me with frank curiosity and came up and stood beside me.

He was a very old man. He must have been more than eighty, and he had all the garrulity which comes with age in rural districts.

'Ole tree nearly done now,' he said, following the direction of my gaze.

'Yes, surely 'tis nearly finished. Her'll have to get another lover soon.'

'Who will?' I asked.

'Her. Down there.' He pointed to the roots of the tree. 'Yes, her'll have to get another lover soon or die. Die proper, I mean, and go to the bad place. And when she be proper dead, ole tree'll die along with her, and soonest best. Her be a toad, blast her!'

And he spat deliberately in the direction of the roots of the tree.

'I don't follow you,' I said, a little shocked at the old man's sudden display of venom.

'The young 'uns thinks they knows too much with all their schoolin', and they won't believe what I tells 'em. But I mind the day, and I seed it with my own eyes. Sixty years ago it was, an' that ole tree looked as near dead as now. And then her down there gets another lover. 'Twas a young gentleman from college whose father lived over to Maid's Rue. And she took 'un. He just faded away and died. A decline they called it, but she took 'un. An' that ole tree, it grew young again, and I never see such a blaze of blossom in the spring. Her lives on men's lives, and her'll go on livin' on 'em until her can't get no more. And then her'll die proper and go to the bad place. Her be worse nor sin and Satan, her be. Well, good marnin', sir. I mus'n be late.'

He shambled on, leaving me alone with no very pleasant thoughts. The tale he told was as impossible as it was ghastly, and I was particularly anxious lest Serringham should hear it while he was undergoing his present phase. Subsequently I breakfasted alone, and I did not see him until after twelve o'clock, when he came downstairs sleepy and unshaven.

'I know you think I'm a lazy brute,' he said, 'but a lot of rest is good for me, and I've been conjuring up the most delightful dreams. You sleep all right?'

'Yes, thanks,' I said. 'By the way, what was that scent I noticed about the house this morning? It seemed to me exactly like may-blossom.'

He laughed shortly.

'Oh, yes, I've noticed that. It puzzled me a bit at first. What do you think it is?'

'I can't guess.'

'That bowl of pot-pourri in the window over there. One notices it first thing in the morning, and then one gets used to it. It's like going into a room laden with tobacco smoke. You smell it as you enter, and as soon as you've been sitting in it a minute, smoking yourself, you can't smell anything at all.'

The explanation seemed reasonable, but later I sniffed at the bowl of pot-pourri. The scent was not in the least like that of may-blossom. On the following morning, the Monday, I drove back to town, and I told Pamela that Serringham was doing very well. But I said it with certain mental reservations.

A month passed, and spring advanced upon the heels of winter. I had news of Serringham through Pamela, but she had never anything much to tell me. I knew intuitively that she was worrying about him, but she would not admit it until one Friday at the end of the month.

'When are you going to see George again?' she asked.

'He hasn't asked me.'

'Oh, you know he doesn't expect you to wait to be asked! Why don't you run down and see him tomorrow? I wish you would.'

'Why?'

'Oh—because—because I don't think that place is doing him any good. He says he's all right, but he's not like his old self in his letters. They're fewer and shorter and, somehow, disjointed and dream-like. I haven't heard from him for nearly a week now, although I've been writing long letters every day. I've tried not to be imaginative about him, but it isn't any good and oh—I wish you'd drive over tomorrow and see him.'

It happened that I was free, but I felt very unwilling to go. Looking back upon that week-end which I had already spent with him, I realised more clearly than ever how little I had enjoyed it. There was something subtly disagreeable in the recollection which I was, and still am, quite incapable of defining or explaining.

'What's the matter with his letters?' I asked, 'apart from the fact that they're fewer and shorter? We're not all ardent and brilliant correspondents, Pam, and I know I should feel the strain if I were expected to write to a girl every day.'

'I wouldn't mind if it were only one word on a postcard. Jack, it's a dreadful thing to say, but he seems to be losing his grip on life. He seems to live in a sort of opium dream. He writes as if he's losing all his old interests—even me. You know what I'm afraid of, my dear, don't you?'

I nodded. I was afraid of the same thing. I had heard before of a nervous breakdown leading to complete mental collapse.

'I don't believe the place suits him,' Pamela continued. 'And it can't be healthy for him to live there all by himself. I was against it from the first, but he wanted to do it, and it seemed best not to try to thwart him. Do go and try to get him away!'

'I'll do my best,' I answered doubtfully.

And so I went.

I reached Maid's Rue late in the afternoon, but it was still daylight. On my way down I could mark the progress of the spring. The hedges were all bare a month since, save for a few pale spears thrusting out their heads on thorny sprays; but a pale mist of green now enveloped them, and primroses were out in the sheltered hollows. Outside Maid's Rue I went right round the triangle in order to turn the car, and saw to my surprise that the hawthorn tree, which had shown not so much as a leaf-bud a month since, was as green now as the roadside hedges. The old tree which had looked to be dead was now making a wonderful, and strange recovery.

I had not warned Serringham of my intended visit, and as I approached the cottage I thought, and hoped, that he had gone away without warning us of his intended departure. The cottage wore an air of desertion, and the illusion was sustained when nobody answered my summons at the door. Even if he had gone out, I argued, Mrs Hickory would be there. And then, just as I was about to return to the car and drive off to make inquiries in the neighbourhood, the door opened very slowly, and Serringham's face peered out at me.

The sight of him shocked me. His eyes were glazed and hollow, his cheeks sunken, his fingers on the doorpost trembled and fidgeted, and he wore at least a week's growth of beard.

'Oh, it's you, is it?' he said in an expressionless voice. 'Come in.'

I followed him into the room which he used as a dining-room, and there he stood, apparently lost in thought for a long minute, his fingers rubbing the stubble on his chin.

'I suppose you'll want some tea,' he said at last, with composed ungraciousness, 'I think I can manage that. There'll be some milk. Yes, they always leave milk.'

'Where's Mrs Hickory?' I asked.

'Mrs Hickory?' He frowned, as if he had some faint recollection of having once heard the name. 'Oh yes, I got rid of her. I was tired of seeing her about the house. I manage better without her. My wants are so simple now.'

'Well, you sit down,' I said, 'and let me forage. I'll get tea for us both.'

He agreed to my suggestion without a word of apology. It was all rather horrible. He was like a drug fiend nearing the end of his body's endurance. But even then I had no idea to what extent he had allowed himself to go to pieces.

I found tea and sugar and milk, but I searched the place in vain for food. I could find only some crusts of bread, very dry and stale, and a little butter already turned sour. And then I knew that the man was starving himself. It took some time to get the kettle to boil, and I was glad, for I wanted to think, and I was in no hurry to face that scarecrow in the next room. That he had been starving himself was self-evident, but I did not suppose that he had done it for a purpose. He had simply been too absorbed in something to trouble about food.

Evidently Serringham had paid me the compliment of throwing me a thought or two, for when I brought in the tea-tray he said:

'I hope you don't want to stay the night. You see, now Mrs Hickory's gone—'

I set down the tray and turned upon him roundly.

'Upon my word, George,' I said, 'you've a nice sense of hospitality!'

'I didn't ask you to come,' he said slowly, unabashed.

'You seem to forget that I'm Pamela's brother.'

I saw a slow smile hide itself amongst the stubble on his face.

'Pamela's brother,' he repeated simply.

'Look here, George,' I exclaimed, 'are you mad?'

'Mad? No. I think I have been learning to be sane.'

'Do you call it sane to starve yourself to death? When did you eat anything last?'

'Yesterday, I think. But it doesn't matter. There is a great deal too much importance attached to food.'

'Rot! Not in your case. And do you know that Pamela's worried to death about you. Why haven't you been writing?'

He looked at me for a moment, and then lowered his gaze without speaking. I turned and began pouring out the tea. He should at least have something hot and wet. He took the cup from my hand and began quite docilely to sip from it.

'Are you going back tonight?' he asked presently, unable to conceal his eagerness to be rid of me.

'If I do, my lad, you're coming too.'

He shook his head at that.

'Oh, no. Certainly not. Quite definitely not. Why should I?'

'Because you're a sick man, and it isn't healthy for you to stay here alone.'

He uttered that dreadful chuckle.

'Alone? Who said I was alone? Eh? Who said that?'

'Well, I don't see anybody else about. And, anyhow, unless my sight deceived me in the larder you can't be entertaining very lavishly.'

Serringham eyed me narrowly.

'There are some sorts of beings to whom food isn't at all necessary,' he said.

'I never heard of any,' I retorted; 'and, anyhow, you're not one of them.'

There was a pause.

'I don't want to argue with you,' he resumed presently, 'but really, you know, you have a great deal to learn. I'm beginning to learn. I began to learn as soon as I arrived here. Slowly, you know. One doesn't make these tremendous discoveries all in half an hour. Do you believe, for instance, that you have ever loved? I tell you that you have not. I tell you that human love, sex love, is but the palest shadow of a mighty substance. There is another love which demands everything, every moment, every thought, every dream. It demands all and gives all, and is all-sufficient.'

'That sounds very pretty,' I said. 'Am I to tell Pamela that?'

He hesitated, but his face and voice were alike shameless and unapologetic.

'Tell Pamela the truth,' he said, and added wearily: 'She keeps on writing to me.'

I kept my temper with him, but I said:

'The truth is, George, that you're as mad as a coot. You've got yourself into this state through sheer accursed loneliness. And I'm going to take you back with me to-morrow—by force, if necessary.'

He shook his head quite passionately but not the less resolutely,

'i could tuck you under one arm,' I reminded him, 'in your present state.'

'Perhaps you could. But that would not stop me from calling for help. You can't abduct people, mad or sane, you know. And I have an idea that, with a little concentration which I should hate to waste, I could convince any medical man that I am as sane as you.'

He had me beaten there, and I knew it. One can't remove people by force from one place to another, even for their own good. My only chance was to get some local medical man to see him and certify him as mad, for mad I now believed him to be.

'Look here,' I said, 'will you eat something if I go out and get it. I'll bring in some cold stuff, and we'll have supper together, and then I'll go.'

He did not object to eating. Clearly he was quite indifferent as to whether he ate or not. His neglect of himself was merely because he would not be troubled to buy and prepare food, nor endure the presence of anybody who would do it for him. But he looked at me with a kind of sly eagerness.

'Yes,' he said, 'that's a good idea. You go out and get some food.'

I knew that he said it because he wanted to be rid of me if only for a little while. He wanted to be alone, but not entirely alone as he had now come to understand solitude. He would spend the time entranced with the creation of his fancy, the imaginary Belle Dame Sans Merci who had him in thrall. The worst trouble was that he was too willing a slave. He was well content to allow his dream to lead him to stupor and death. I still called it a dream, you see.

I left him in peace for a while and drove the car down into Hazelsea, where I laid in a store of cooked meats and other provisions. I also called on a medical man, selecting the owner of the first brass plate I saw. Dr Green, a dapper, cheerful, middle-aged man, listened to me and nodded comprehendingly from time to time.

'It's a difficult case,' he said, 'I'll go and look him up tomorrow if I can get him to see me. Of course, I can't say that a man is mad merely because he is eccentric and chooses to lead the life of a hermit. I might agree with you that it would be far better for him to be taken away and put under medical care, but I can't compel him to go unless I see symptoms of undoubted insanity. It's a risky business for a doctor to certify a man as mad, and rightly so. However, I'll go and see him and let you know what I think if you'll leave me your address. Meanwhile, if you're anxious about his neglecting altogether to eat, the only thing you can do is to leave a standing order with the shops for provisions to be sent up to him.'

There was sound sense in that last suggestion and before returning to the cottage I left money for a month's supply of food at the local stores.

On my return I found the door undone and walked in. Serringham sat huddled up in the dusk in a deep armchair and scarcely moved as I entered.

The room was heavy with perfume—the perfume of may-blossom. I recoiled from the atmosphere as from a blast of heat. I had always loved that heavy sweet odour, that innocent scent of the English hedgerows in May-time, so suggestive of youth and love and all the sweeter things of life; but now it nauseated me and vaguely frightened me. The time was March, remember, and the leaves scarcely out. And I remembered the words of the old man who had spoken to me by the hawthorn tree outside.

'Where does that confounded smell come from?' I asked roughly of Serringham.

He did not answer the question, but stared dazedly across the room.

'She has grey-green eyes,' he muttered, 'like the sea under storm-clouds.'

'Who has?' I demanded; and I felt a sudden sweat of horror in the roots of my hair.

'You know!' he murmured. 'They buried her poor body out yonder at the cross-roads. But they buried only the husk of her as in due time they will bury only the husk of me. I have little use for my husk, having learned that there are passions of the spirit. You, too, may learn in time. You have learned a little already, I think . . .'

His voice trailed away, and I know that the face I turned upon him must have been a face of horror.

'For pity's sake,' I cried, 'for your sake, and Pamela's and mine, pull yourself together just for one moment and listen. I thought that the worst that could be happening to you was that you were going mad. And now I'm not so sure. There may be worse than that. Try to think clearly. I know what is in your mind now—or, rather, I am afraid to know. There may be worse than that. Try to think clearly. I know nothing about these things, George; I suppose even now I don't believe in them—try to think how this must end. It's leading you to death, and worse than death.'

He sighed wearily.

'What is death?' he asked, 'I thought you were beginning to know better. Oh, go away and leave me to my happiness.'
But I made him eat before I went. He ate listlessly and rather unwillingly, and all the while his eyes looked yearningly about the room. I confess that I wasn't sorry to go. To me the cottage and its visible occupant had become a place of terror.

I told Pamela the truth as kindly as I could; or that part of the truth which alone I admitted to myself in broad daylight. Lurking in my mind were things which I dared not seek out and try to visualise.

'I'm afraid his mental condition is unsound,' I had to tell her, 'but we can't do anything until we hear from the doctor. If he insists on staying there, and the verdict is that he is sane enough to be allowed to do so, I am afraid we can't do anything.'

On the Tuesday I heard from Dr Green, and his letter contained just such a report as I had feared I should receive. He had been to see Serringham, and Serringham—I could imagine his pulling himself together for the interview—had seemed perfectly reasonable, i found him neurotic and undernourished, but I should not care to say more than that, nor did I see the least reason for putting him under restraint. He admitted that he had somewhat neglected himself, but he promised to mend his ways in that respect. All I can do is to let you know if I hear of any change. His manner made it quite impossible for me to call on him again without invitation.'

Pamela bore it very bravely. It seemed dreadful to leave him to his fate, but it comforted her to know that food was being left daily for him at the cottage. She continued to write to him daily without receiving any reply.

Afterwards some forty or fifty of her letters were found unopened.

But one day in April she came to me in tears.

'I can't bear it any longer,' she said. 'I must see him whether he wants me or not, and whether he loves me or hates me. Perhaps if I were to see him and plead with him it might make a difference—it might get him to return with us and leave that awful solitude which is turning his brain. Do drive me down to him.'

It was a prospect which I need not have dreaded, for the house was silent and the doors securely fastened when we arrived, nor did all my beating on the door summon the solitary inmate.

'Perhaps he's gone out,' Pamela suggested drearily at last. I could think of nothing more unlikely, but I welcomed her suggestion.

'Let's go away for a little while,' she said next, 'and then come back and see if he's in.'

So we turned away and went to the gate, and at the gate we both stopped and looked back at the house. Serringham, unkempt and terribly haggard, stood in one of the front windows, watching our departure with a smirk of satisfaction. Pamela cried out at once and waved a hand, whereupon he withdrew himself quickly out of sight.

She turned to me, caught my arm and hugged it, and her lips were trembling. 'You're quite right,' she said dully. 'We can't do anything. He doesn't want me anymore. Take me away, please, Jack.'

The hawthorn tree at the cross-roads was now in full leaf. Pamela sat looking at it while I started up the car, and spoke, I know, for the mere sake of speaking.

'What a lovely tree that will be when the blossom comes out,' she said in a small, tremulous voice.

'Yes,' I agreed with a shudder; 'and a couple of months ago it looked as if it were dying.'

Serringham was found dead in the cottage towards the middle of May. He was found lying on the floor of the dining-room, with his arms outstretched, as if he had fallen in the act of trying to embrace something which had eluded him. No milk or provisions had been taken into the house for days, and eventually the police broke in to make the tragic discovery. The post-mortem revealed the fact that he had died simply through malnutrition.

I went down for the funeral and to shut up the cottage. The hawthorn tree at the cross-roads was now a mass of red blossom. The policeman who accompanied me to Maid's Rue pointed it out to me.

'That's a wonderful old tree,' he remarked. 'Looks just as if it's had a new life given to it this year.'

'Yes,' I agreed, 'it looks just as if it's had new life given to it this year.'

The Ivory Cards

From the age of two, and until I was turned twelve, I saw little of my mother. I was the posthumous son of a father who followed a humble trade and who left my mother almost penniless; so that after a little while she returned to service in the great house in which she had formerly been a maid.

Fortunately for me, there was a well-endowed charity connected with my father's trade, and in due time I went to an institute which provided me with a bed, board, and education for ten months in the year. For the holidays I went to my uncle, who kept a baker's shop in Hounslow; and it was only during occasional brief flying visits to the school or to her brother's house that my mother was able to see me.

Some years before my twelfth birthday my mother had risen to be housekeeper to Sir George Suttwell, at his great house in Hampshire, and had—I don't know how many— servants under her. She was one of those strong, honest, capable women, especially designed by nature for filling humble positions of trust. Most people stood in awe of her, and I think the only two beings she feared under heaven were Sir George and his lady. For them she had a respect amounting almost to reverence, and worshipped the family as if she had been some feudal serf born and bred on the estate. It was this attitude towards her employers which kept us apart for so long. She was afraid to ask for permission to have me with her during holidays, deeming that I, being a boy, would be certain to do something which would bring down the wrath from Olympus on both of us. So, as I grew towards my teens, my mother remained a beloved stranger, a great lady whose periodical visitations quelled the humdrum chatter of my uncle and aunt with allusions to hunt balls, society weddings, and such-like things which, for all I was able to realise, might have been taking place on the planet Mars.

Although I loved my mother, as was natural, and always looked forward to seeing her, I was happy enough with my uncle and aunt when I was not at school. My uncle, good man, was of that simple nature which can seek and find companionship in a child. He was a stay-at-home man, his only pleasure outside his own back-parlour being to watch football matches; and even then he used to take me with him when I was at home.

He had taught me ecarte and cribbage, and played at one or the other with me in the evenings in the parlour behind the shop. It was to my knowledge of the first of these games that I came afterwards to owe my better education, my modest fortune, and my start in life. And the story of that rubber of ecarte which won me a place in life high above the station in which I was born, is one which I shall blame no man for taking leave to doubt.

I had turned twelve years old by a month or two, and was nearly thirteen, when those eventful Easter holidays came round.

Sir George and Lady Suttwell were elderly folk who rarely left their house in Hampshire for longer than a weekend. But that spring some necessary renovations in the house were driving them away for a time, and my mother had plucked up courage to ask if she might have me with her.

And I was actually to go. See Suttwell Court and die, my mother had always seemed to hint; so please imagine the state of excitement into which I worked myself.

Suttwell Court stands on the westward fringe of the New Forest, and four good miles by road from Farringhurst Station. I remember the train, after it left Southampton, taking me through stretches of the forest agleam in the sun with the first pale vivid greens of spring. But the sun was low in the sky when I stepped out on Farringhurst platform, and a dense April rain-cloud, stealing up out of the west, drew a gloomy curtain across the day's end. I was met by my mother, kissed, and led by her to a ramshackle bus which had served for a generation as a means of transport for luggage and servants. For most of the way sharp arrows of rain rattled the windows and beat upon the roof, and this gloomy end to a bright day, added to the fact that I was tired after my journey, probably tended to depress me and to weigh down my mind with all manner of shapeless and unreasonable forebodings.

I know that I had a strange, perverse dread of the house when I looked out of the window and first saw it, while the warm rain beat down upon my bare head. I had imagined Suttwell Court to be modelled on a palace in an Oriental fairy tale, only to see that it was larger and even gloomier than the institute in which I had spent most of my life. I entered it with the same sense of awe with which a child may be made to enter a cathedral.

A supper of sausages in my mother's sitting-room did something towards cheering me. A very affable gentleman, named Mr Hewitt, shared the meal with us. I learnt from my mother that he was the butler; and thenceforth in my assessment of social values butlers stood little if anything lower than the House of Peers. He seemed to me to have more dignity and more humour, and an easier condescension towards a twelve-year-old than any of the masters at the orphanage.

My mother packed me off early to bed, but before doing so she showed me over a little, a very little, of those parts of the house which were sacred at normal times. Then my awe and depression returned together. Everything was alarmingly big and massive; there was not a picture that did not seem to be twenty times the size of an ordinary picture, hardly a chair in which a giant might not have sat in comfort. The very carpets under my feet were an embarrassment; they were so thick and beautiful that I expected at any moment to be blamed for walking on them.

I was grateful for the fact that my bedroom lay at the end of a corridor which seemed the homeliest corner of the house, being carpeted with coconut matting, and my room itself had linoleum on the floor, and some thin, worn rugs, which reminded me comfortably of Hounslow and the sitting-room at Uncle Fred's.

My spirits improved on the following day, and the house seemed less terrifying in the morning light, when, accompanied by my mother, I completed my tour of the house. My mother, very brisk and business-like, moved to the sound of a perpetual rattling of keys, and this somehow imbued me with a sense of her importance, so that I was more in awe of her than ever. She never had to look twice for a key, nor made any error in selecting the right one. And she had some brief comment on every room we entered, pointing out a rare piece of furniture or an interesting picture, or telling of some important family matter which had taken place there.

I suppose the pictures interested me more than anything else. There were many portraits of ancestors, particularly in the hall and in the long gallery upstairs. The family likeness between these Suttwells was most marked, and if my mother had not been by to tell me differently, I might easily have imagined that the portraits were all of the one man taken in different costumes and at different periods of his life. The richness and beauty of their dresses gripped my imagination, and never having seen the present Sir George, I half-imagined that he worked abroad in a powdered wig and brocaded coat, with a rapier at his side. Having listened to my mother it was impossible to imagine him as other men.

Only one room did we pass unvisited on our tour through the house, and that because it was the one room which was kept locked and of which my mother had not the key. This locked door was on the first floor, on a corridor running direct from the main staircase to the west wing, and my curiosity was naturally aroused when my mother would have whisked me past it.

'But what's inside it?' I asked.

'I don't know,' my mother returned shortly.

'But why haven't you the key?'

'Sir George has that. I suppose he knows his own business best.'

I think my mother was displeased because the key of this room had not been entrusted to her along with the other keys, and this had the effect of making her shorter than usual in answering my questions. Having an imagination and a taste for lurid literature you may imagine how this locked room took a grip on my fancy. There had been a murder committed there.

The skeleton of a man still lay among his own mouldering finery. There was still a great bloodstain in the middle of the floor. But my mother was impatient and very discouraging when I hinted at these awesome but delightful possibilities.

The house would have been an ideal playground for me had I been allowed to use it as such, but I was confined to my mother's room and the great kitchen, although sometimes the kindly Mr Hewitt allowed me to help him dust the glasses in his pantry. Out of doors it was almost as bad. The gardens were held even more sacred to the feet than was the great, grey carpet in the long drawing-room.

But the servants, indoor and out, were alike friendly, and seemed to enjoy spoiling me when my mother was not looking. Not all of them held the family in such reverence as did my mother, and from Mr Sturgess, who was one of the gardeners and never too busy to talk, I learned a great deal more family history than my mother cared to tell me. It was he who took my breath away by informing me that Sir George was a poor man. I winked to show that I was not so easily to be taken in.

'I don't mean as you and I mightn't like to change places with him,' Mr Sturgess confessed. 'But he ain't rich according to his own ideas. Not what gentry call rich. When you sees the woods all thinned out and the guv'nor selling land a bit at a time, it means only one thing. The gentry aren't getting very fat on the land nowadays. I'm thinking that if Sir George's old father was still alive the family would have had to have packed up from here before now.'

And then he told me that for many generations in the Suttwell family the heads of the house had been misers and spendthrifts alternately. One man had drained the estate and left it in debt; his son had followed him and improved the family fortunes, only for the succeeding generation to spend recklessly again.

'Old Sir Hugh, Sir George's old father, was a spendthrift if ever there was one,' Sturgess informed me.

'And is this Sir George a miser, then?' I asked.

Sturgess grinned and scratched his chin.

'Well, perhaps it wouldn't do to call him that,' he said. 'But he's close—he's devilish close!'

My first five days at Suttwell Court passed pleasantly and uneventfully enough. I dare say I should have been bored most of the time had not some of the servants deigned to play with me; and I earned Mr Hewitt's respect by teaching him how to play ecarte.

'The best game of nap for two that's ever been invented,' was his verdict on the game.

It was on the sixth evening of my stay at Suttwell Court that the thing happened.

My mother, strong disciplinarian that she was, would permit no late hours for me. At half-past nine every night I was kissed, given my candle, and pushed to the door. Always, within half an hour, I heard her enter the room adjoining mine.

The workmen were still in strong force during the daytime, and some of them were engaged on work on the back staircase, so that on this particular night we could not use it. I was told to go through the hall and up the main staircase on my way to bed.

It was a dark night outside, moonless and starless, and the house was plunged in almost total darkness. I remember the funny, awesome shadows made by my progress through the hall with my little candle, and how the eyes of the portraits stared at me through the penumbra, as if indignantly wondering what right I had to be there. The shadows about me sagged and swelled as I made my way up the staircase, and I was glad to reach the top and get away from the focuses of those many eyes on the walls below.

I had taken half a dozen steps down the corridor leading to the west wing, when I suddenly stopped. I had come to the door of that mysterious locked room, and I had to stand and stare at it for a spell, as a child without the money to enter a show will stand and feast its eyes upon the outside. I could not have stood there more than a moment or two. I was about to pass on when there happened that which I know so well to be true and still seems to me so incredible.

Without any warning, but without any noise which startled me, the door opened. There was a gentleman standing on the threshold, and behind him the room was lit up. I fell back a step and stared. I was certainly surprised, but I was not flung into such a state of stupefaction as might have been expected, and, quite strangely, I was not afraid.

The gentleman was smiling. His face was round and bloated, but, withal, good-humoured, and there was a sort of glassy-smile in his eyes which I had seen before on men who were good-natured in their cups. The man looked tipsy, but he looked amiable. His whole aspect was so friendly that it disarmed fear on the instant.

'Why,' he said in a soft, throaty voice, 'it's a boy! Here, boy!'

I took a step towards him, holding my candle low. He was beautifully dressed in what I afterwards described to my mother as a fancy costume—like one of the portraits in the hall. With the strong Suttwell family likeness which was his, he might have passed for any one of them. He wore lace at his throat and wrists, and a long skirted coat of a most beautiful shade of blue. Beneath the hem of it on his left, I saw a long, thin scabbard protruding. A wig, curled and heavily powdered, hid his natural hair.

I am thankful that it did not occur to me then to think what I know now. He looked as solid and actual as anybody I had ever seen; and the portraits had given my simple young mind to think that the Suttwells still walked abroad in their wigs and Georgian finery. He was one of those demi-gods reverently referred to as 'the family'. I just grinned at him shyly, and, I dare say, engagingly, wondering how he had come to return home without my mother, who knew everything, being aware of it.

'Where are you going, boy?' he asked.

'Please, sir, to bed.'

'Oh, to Hades with bed!' He had a petulant little mincing voice which came strangely from one of his height and girth, the fashionable drawl of the seventeen-eighties. 'Come, now, you'll be so obliging as to spare me a little of your company. I get little company now.'

There was a note of sadness in his voice as he uttered these last words, and I found myself feeling sorry for him. Then he said something in French which I could not understand, but which I took to be an invitation to enter the room, especially as he stood a little to one side as he spoke.

I entered the room, he withdrawing just in front of me. It was quite brightly lit without the light which I had brought in with me, but how I cannot now tell. I do not remember seeing lamp or candles. The apartment was some kind of living-room. There was a table in the middle, solid old chairs, books, a bureau; and the dust of ages lay thick over everything.

'Yes,' he said, 'I have little company now, and I am not fain to be too particular. It was otherwise once. I vow I have been starving for longer than I care to think for a deal o' the cards.' He grinned at me slyly, as a gentleman will who lures a boy into harmless mischief. 'I take it ye wouldn't be a card-player?' he said.

'Yes, sir,' I answered back, 'I play some games.'

His smile broadened and then he shook his head.

'Some game of the tap-room and stables, I doubt not,' he said. 'Well, well, better small beer than plain water, I suppose. 'Twill be a real pleasure to feel the cards in my hands again. Well, what's your tap-room swindle? Name it, boy!'

I hardly understood him, but I said:

'Please, sir, I can play ecarte.'

'Play ecarte!' The grin on his lips broadened and his eyes seemed to grow wider as if with pleasure and surprise. 'Play ecarte! Why, 'tis the great game at White's at this very hour! Now, who the devil has been lessoning this brat in such polite accomplishments?'

He spoke as if to himself, and then became mightily civil, making me a bow so ironical and amusing that I was tempted to laugh rather than to feel hurt.

'Sir,' said he, 'I am deeply honoured and obileeged by your company, and if ye play ecarte you are double welcome. I have lost more pieces at ecarte than my brat—rot him!—will ever win back with all his copy-book virtues. If you will honour me with a game'

He eyed me as anxiously as if he thought I dared refuse. I said nothing, but simply stood looking at him with my puzzled nervous smile.

I found my assent taken for granted, and he went to the bureau, opened a drawer, and took out a pack of playing cards. These he dropped on to the middle of the dust-laden table.

'I take it,' he said, eyeing me with his lazy, slightly tipsy, and whimsical smile, 'that we shall play for the usual club stakes?'

I guessed him to be chaffing me, after the manner of a fine gentleman whose dignity would permit him to take nothing from a boy. Indeed, I had nothing to lose, but I was sure that if I won this kind, eccentric gentleman would not send me away empty-handed. So I grinned and said, 'Yes,' although to be truthful I was beginning to be nervous.

'Will you cut?' said he, and indicated the cards with a bow of genuine ceremony.

The pack was already 'stripped' for ecarte, which is to say that it consisted of only thirty-two cards, the lowest being the sevens. It was while I was cutting that I noticed for the first time the great beauty and rarity of the cards; for they were of ivory, hand-painted and treated by some process which made the colours durable. I lost the deal and drew up a chair to the table. 'A rubber of three games?' asked the gentleman.

I nodded, and he began to deal, and as he did so I noticed that his manner had changed. The playfulness was all gone out of him. As soon as he touched the cards a painful and—to me— terrifying seriousness took possession of him. The mark of one of his besetting sins was stamped on his face for a child to read.

We began to play. He handled his little fan of cards with shaking fingers. He declined my request for cards, declared the King of trumps, and won two points of the hand. He won the first game by scoring five points to my two.

I was beginning to be frightened, although I could not have said why. But fortune favoured me in the second game, and I scored my five while he could show only three. I was nervous enough, but he seemed even more so when he picked up the cards to deal the first hand in the final game.

And what a game that was! No hand produced more than one point, and we scored alternately until the score was four all. He had the cards; spades were trumps; and I looked up fearfully from a bad hand into his pale prominent bloodshot eyes.

'Do you give cards?' I asked.

He hesitated, and then nodded. I asked for four. He dealt them out one by one, and the first I picked up was the King of Spades.

'I hold the King,' said I, with a little gasp of relief, and thrust it out towards him.

He sprang up with an oath, dashing his own cards on to the table so violently that I sprang back in alarm, still clutching in my hand the King of Spades.

' 'Tis the kind of luck has always dogged me,' he said, in a quieter tone.

And with that he began to pace the room, with his head held very low, so that I wondered if he were joking and if he expected me to smile at him. Then presently he came to a halt and stared hard at me.

'Boy,' said he, 'I am vastly obleeged for your entertainment. And what do you say if I cannot pay you?'

Again I wondered if he were chaffing me.

'Please sir,' I said, 'it doesn't matter.'

Strangely enough, my answer seemed to annoy him.

'Oho,' said he, 'and I am much obleeged for your forbearance, Master Stable-boy, and rot your impudence! There's no man living or dead can say that Giles Suttwell ever compounded a gaming-debt. Rot your impudence! Do you hear me? Rot your impudence!'

In a moment he had worked himself up into a rage, leaning over the table ferociously, and glaring at me, and I found myself tongue-tied with fright so that I could not even stammer a word of apology.

He fell to pacing the room again, head down, and muttering to himself. Then presently he stopped again and stared at me.

'Rot your damned impudence! But how to pay ye—ay, there's the rub!'

He stood considering, and then to my relief moved on one side and left me a free passage to the door.

'I'll wish you a good evening,' he said, 'I'm vastly obileeged for your company. I'm sure. And rot your impudence.'

I ran to the door. He followed me a step or two behind.

'You'll pay yourself, boy,' I heard him say. 'What was my father's is mine, although the damned old skinflint hid it from me and from those who followed. The library ... the fifth panel behind the shelves on the left of the south door . . . take what is due. . . .'

I was outside the room and I turned to look at him as his voice behind me died away. I was staring straight at a closed door. Then a great terror came upon me, and I fled down the stairs, crying aloud, through the great kitchen, and into my mother's arms. I understood little then, but my terror told me that I had been with something that was not of the earth and was not holy.

My mother, who tried to pacify me, would never have believed a word of what I had to tell if she had not noticed that I clutched something convulsively in one of my hands. Then she made me unclose my fingers, and took from them an ivory card. It was the King of Spades.

My mother took the risk of keeping me until Sir Charles and his lady returned. To them I told my story, and the ivory card was shown. They said little. Not until long afterwards did I learn that the locked room which I had visited had been shut up because it was reputed to be haunted by a Sir Giles Suttwell, who had gambled away his substance and drank himself to death towards the end of the eighteenth century.

The room was opened and a pack of thirty-one ivory cards was found in the bureau—a pack complete for ecarte save for the King of Spades. And because a boy cannot enter a locked room and take a card from a locked bureau, having the key to neither, great attention was paid to my story and particularly to the end of it.

Before Sir Giles the spendthrift had come Sir Giles the miser. I do not know the number of guineas found in a secret room behind the shelves in the library. I only know that my mother and I must thank Sir George for having had our share of them.

Little Bride-of-a-Day

'You don't mind, sir,' said old George Brooks, the landlord, 'I'll get you to put your name down in the book. We don't often have folk staying here, 'specially at this time o' the year, and I mostly forgets it, but I believe 'tis still the law.'

He rose from his seat at the opposite chimney comer and went out. While he was gone I stirred the peat fire with my heel and invented a likely-sounding alias. I could see that he did not know me—twenty years had wrought more than the usual changes in my appearance— and it was not convenient for me to reveal my identity to him.

It was a wild night, and the wind, shrieking over Dartmoor, buffeted in vain the inn which had withstood such onslaughts for close upon five hundred years. The red curtains which hid the trembling shutters were kept perpetually astir by strong currents of air which found their way in between the chinks. Every window in the house was rattling, and the smoke which tried to find an outlet through the wide chimney was blown back into the room in gusts. Indeed, a dark mist of pungent smoke pervaded the room, and pictures on the far wall looked vague and indistinct from the comer where I sat.

I knew that little tap-room with its dingy settles, plain deal tables and tiled floor, for I had good reason to remember it. As it had been twenty years ago, so it was today. The same pictures were on the walls, only a very little dirtier. They were mostly old Christmas number plates, and I knew them from memory: the monks laughing over 'Punch', 'Bubbles', the Charge of the Guards at Inkerman, 'Sambo's Christening'—all in their old places and burned into my memory as if with branding-irons. I had thought I remembered every detail of that day, but the sight of these things awakened a host of sleeping memories—little things which were so nearly nothings and yet hurt inexpressibly to recall.

During those minutes while I was alone I sat and wondered what had brought me there. I did not want to start an old lesion; that wound was healed, or so I told myself. A man cannot always be grieving over an irrevocable loss; Nature has decreed otherwise. I had been happy in my fashion for so many years, feeling only in occasional lonely moments that dreary little ache of the heart which reminds one so inexplicably of the wail of a violin. I had been content to drug my memory, using such distractions as had seemed good to me, but I had never really forgotten. That is why I was there tonight.

And what had brought me? A chance word overheard, first of all, followed by a silly-season article in a Sunday paper about strange happenings in a Devon inn. The inn was not named, and even the district was carefully concealed, but I knew that I knew it. And then I heard something at the club, one member holding forth to another close beside me.

Oh, the first member was quite certain that it was true. The experience belonged to a friend of his who, he was assured, was incapable of lying. No, he didn't quite know where the inn was, save that it was somewhere in Devon, but he could probably find out. Was there any story attached to the inn—had any tragedy happened there—to account for it? Oh, yes. It had happened about a hundred years ago ... a runaway couple, you know . . . and the girl had died there.

A hundred years ago! It had happened only twenty! The story was already a legend, garbled, twisted, distorted beyond any recognition save mine. But listening to the man I knew beyond doubt the name of the inn, and, had I chosen, I could have corrected him in half a hundred details. I listened with such emotions as the ghost of a man might feel who reads his own epitaph.

But I was less concerned with the whole story, which I knew too well, than with the report that strange things had ever since happened at the inn.

The old pain was only drugged and not killed. It wakened again, and with it there opened up before me new avenues of hope. Suppose, after all, it were true that death is not the last phase of humanity, but a mere change of circumstances! Suppose a sign awaited me in the house which I had never revisited for fear of torturing myself! Well, I took my chance, and that is why tonight saw me back again in the Crooked Fiddler.

Old George Brooks returned with his hotel register, which was a plain, black-covered exercise book. In it I scribbled my fictitious name and an imaginary address in Kensington. Old George examined my handwriting and then raised his glass to me.

'Well, Mr Prentice,' said he, 'I'm glad to see you, and here's hearty welcome.'

It was not yet closing time, but we were alone in the tap-room. Only two or three cottages were in the immediate neighbourhood, and the weather was too foul for distant customers to be attracted. He leaned over the fire and shot me quick, inquisitive glances when he thought I was not looking. There was nothing of recognition in his gaze; he was naturally and plainly wondering what had brought a stranger to stay in his house at that season of the year.

I wanted to make him talk, but I was chary of arousing his suspicions.

The silence between us dragged on until I coughed.

'Reckon you've got this smoke In your throat, sir,' he then said. 'There's a nice fire in your sitting-room, sir—a coal fire—and one of them modern grates.'

'As a matter of fact,' I said, smiling, 'I want company. I'd sooner sit here, if you don't mind.'

He brightened at once.

'Oh, you're kindly welcome, sir. I'm glad enough to have company. 'Tis mortal lonely here, especially on a night like this. Just hark to the wind!'

As he spoke a gust heavier than ever went raving around the house. It drove a cloud of smoke back from the chimney into our faces. Somewhere a door banged, and mine host started and sat rigid for a moment with the air of one listening.

'I shall never sleep through this,' I murmured.

George Brooks' air of tension relaxed. I could read him sufficiently to know that he had assured himself that the wind was the cause of that door banging, and that he was relieved. He belonged to that strong, hearty, bucolic type which one never associates with nerves; but the nerves were there underneath the bronze and brawn.

'Better keep your head under the clothes, sir,' he said. 'You won't hear so much then. And you've a nice comfortable room.'

'Which is my room?'

'The one over this, sir.'

'Ah, I'd sooner have the other—the one opposite across the passage. Nobody's sleeping in it, because I took the liberty of looking in to see.'

The old man shot me a covert glance and looked away.

'Bedding ain't aired, sir,' he muttered,

'I don't mind carrying it across.'

He was silent a moment, staring down at the mound of smouldering peat.

'Mattress ain't been slept on for a long time, sir. You'd die of rheumatics.'

'I'm willing to risk that.'

My obstinacy plainly worried him and aroused his suspicions,

'I'd as like you didn't have that room,' he said slowly.

'But why?'

'We never do use it now.'

'That's rather a pity. I've taken a fancy to that room.'

The old man knocked out his clay pipe, glanced at me for a moment, and proceeded slowly to refill it.

'I don't want to tell you why I'd rather you didn't have it,' he said.

'You're a gentleman from London and maybe you'd laugh. Maybe you'd laugh less if you slept there. But the brewers don't like me to talk, for they think it doesn't do the house good. Still, whatever room you have you'll maybe see her, for 'tisn't only one place she keeps. But she won't hurt 'ee, sir, you can lay to that.'

'What's this?' I asked, feigning incredulity. 'A ghost?'

'Sounds silly to call her that, sir. But I dunno what else to call her.'

I felt my heart beating hard.

'And she's to be seen in that room opposite mine?'

'Mostly. But she's sometimes all over the house.'

I busied myself for a moment in lighting a cigarette. When I was sure that I had my voice under control, I said, 'I'm not laughing at you. I want to hear about this. What sort of—of ghost is she?'

'A girl, sir; or, rather, a young lady.'

'And you see her often?'

'Yes, often, sir. 'Tis hard to believe, I know. She never takes no notice of us. 'Tisn't us she wants. Sometimes she comes round peeping into all the rooms, like as if she was looking for something. I reckon 'tis her husband she's looking for.'

'Did he—did he leave her, then?'

'No, sir. I suppose in a sense, she left him. You see, she died.'

'And you think she still—wants him?' I asked, almost in a whisper.

'I dunno what else to think. There's something troubles her, poor soul.'

I drew my chair an inch or two closer to the fire and asked, 'What does she look like?'

'She's dressed just as she was when I last saw her. She don't look like a ghost in any of the pictures. If you saw her casual-like for the first time you mightn't know that she wasn't mortal flesh—except you'd get a funny feeling in your bones which made you look again, and then you'd know.'

A sudden chill struck through me.

'You knew her when she was alive, then?' I muttered, 'I'd like to hear about that. '

George Brooks nodded.

'I thought you'd come to that, sir,' he said, 'I've told the story 'bout a thousand times, till I a'most know my own words by heart. It happened twenty years ago—twenty years last April. I was out across the road, feeding the chickens, when a motor-car came humming up to my door. There wasn't near so many on the roads in them days, and to see one around here was still a bit of a novelty. Well, out gets a young gentleman and a young lady, as pretty a couple as you could wish to see, except that the young lady was looking tired and ill. I found out afterwards they'd been married that very morning, but when I first clapped eyes on 'em I guessed 'em for a honeymoon couple. It was a runaway match, as it happened, for it all came out in the papers afterwards, besides the little Mr Harford told me. Mr and Mrs Harford they was, and she called him Paul, and he called her Hesper. And they asked me if they could stay a day or two, and I said "Yes".

'Well, from what I can make out about it, it was this: the gentleman wasn't so high up in the world as the young lady, and there'd been all manner of rows as soon as it was out that they wanted to get married. The young lady's father owned a lot o' land in the middle o' Dorset, and this Mr Harford was sub-agent on his estate until he got dismissed for looking as high as his master's daughter. She wasn't strong; you could see she was one of them frail, clinging, nervous kind, and from what I hear she'd had a hell's own time at home for a full year, bein' bullied and ratted to give him up. I reckon she spent about the last ounce of her strength in sticking to him. So, in the end, he settled matter by runnin' away with her—but he left it too late, poor chap.

'As I've told 'ee, I could see she was ill, but I never guessed—no more nor Mr Harford—how ill she was. Reckon he thought, poor man, as she'd bloom again now she was married to him and away from the nagging tongues of her folk. I'll never forget that night as long as I live. 'Twas close on supper-time.

Mrs Harford was up in the bedroom doing her hair, and Mr Harford was in this very room, as happy as ever I've seen a man in this world. 'Twas easy to tell he was a bridegroom, and I'd been on the point of axing him a dozen times, but didn't quite like. There was half a dozen customers in here—they're mostly still alive—and we was drinking Mr Harford's health, knowing in our own minds as we was drinking the health of bride and bridegroom. And sudden-like we heard a fall upstairs, and Mr Harford rushed up to see what it was.

'I don't like to remember what happened just after that. He didn't get to her in time. When I saw her she was lying there on the floor with her long silky hair over her shoulders. I never knew before as a grown woman could look so like a little child when she was dead.

'Mr Harford never came inside the house again. We reckon he must have spent two nights out on the moor. Like a madman he was. But he must have wired to her father, because he came down for the funeral, and then Mr Harford stayed a couple o' nights in old Jake Blagdon's cottage. There was trouble when Mr Harford and the father met. Mr Harford, he spurned him for having murdered his own daughter. But later on the two men shook hands over the grave. I reckon there wasn't a dry eye in the village that night.'

Just then I found that the smoke had got into my own eyes, and I looked quickly away.

'It's that darned fire!' I muttered.

George Brooks made matters worse by kicking the peat.

'That's all the story,' he said, 'except—except what still happens.'

'What does she—want?' I stammered huskily.

'How would I know? She never speaks, though there are some as swears they've heard her speak and ask for Paul. I reckon she's looking for him—for her husband. Likely enough, when her time came, she found herself going, and called out to him, but he didn't hear.

Maybe, if he'd only stayed in the house that night she'd have managed to say to him what she wanted to say. But he never came back. I never heard what became of him.'

There was a long pause,

'I think I can tell you,' I said at last.

The old man looked up sharply.

'I happen to know a Paul Harford,' I said quickly. 'Very likely it's the same. He's a man of forty-four now.'

'That 'ud be about his age. He was about your height, though not so stout, and he was clean-shaven, and your hair must have been about the same colour before it got a bit grey— if you'll excuse me, sir.'

'That's the man,' said I, keeping my gaze lowered.

'Well, now, to think of that! And how's he getting on, sir?'

'Oh, I think he'd complain of little. I knew he'd had some trouble, and that may account for his way of life. He came into some money—I suppose just a little too late. Most things in this world seem to happen a little too late. I dare say he thinks he's forgotten Hesper, and perhaps he did half succeed. For twenty years is twenty years, and no man could spend twenty years of such suffering as he must have endured for a time. But in learning to forget her he forgot much more besides. He clutched at little moments, at odd half-hours, of hectic pleasure, seeking such poisonous drugs as indeed drugged him in the end. Through the world he went, caring for nobody but himself—for none else was left for him to care for— seeking his own ruin as better men have tried to seek their God. And he drank hard and gambled hard, for in these pleasures there is forgetfulness. And other women came into his life, and with these he played at love as a child plays with toys, knowing that none of them was worth more than a passing thought, and knowing that he had no longer any honest love to offer. And I suppose these toys will last him until the end, for the man he is today is not the boy of twenty years ago. For you see he was a coward who held himself not strong enough to suffer, and that should be his epitaph—if truth ever came to be written upon a tombstone.'

The old man bent his head. I do not suppose he understood more than a half of what I had said.

'Well, now, I'm sorry to hear that,' he said simply.

We sat silent for a little while. Strangely enough, now that I had heard sufficient to justify the wild, unreasonable hope which had sent me there, I was further than ever from believing. I recoiled on the brink of realisation. As I had not dared to suffer, so now I did not dare to believe. The stronger the evidence, the less I gave it credit. But I knew that proof or disproof awaited me during the next few hours. Presently I rose, assuming an air of elaborate carelessness and affecting to yawn.

'I think,' I said, i shall go to bed. I'm tired.'

Old George Brooks rose cumbersomely upon his legs,

'I'll go and get your candle, sir,' he said.

I went first of all to the room which had been prepared for me. I undressed, got into bed, and lay there in the dark until I knew that the small household was at rest. I heard old George Brooks come up, and saw the light from the lamp he carried pierce the chinks of my door as he came past. He slept in the next room to mine, and a little later I heard through the wall the creaking of the springs as he climbed into bed. I strained my ears for further sounds, and, hearing none, at last guessed him to be asleep.

The wind was still raging outside. My window was open, and gusts of cold air played around me. When at last I got out of bed and relit my candle, I had to shield the match with my hands until it was half burned. The wick of the candle was short, and caught only a small bluish flame which needed shielding from the draught.

Moving as guiltily as a thief I crept out of my room and across the landing. Opposite my door I opened another, and found myself facing a shuttered window across a small square room. An odour of damp and desuetude greeted me as I crossed the threshold, and in the meagre light I carried I saw the room which was to have been my bridal chamber.

In twenty years this room had scarcely changed, save that now a hideous patchwork quilt adorned the old oak bed with the tall hangings. I thought I knew the picture of the little girl saying her grace before breakfast in bed with a fox terrier at her elbow in an attitude of reverence. Such small things linger in a man's memory. The bed and the dressing-table, backed against opposite walls, left only a narrow passage between them. Standing before the mirror on the dressing-table, Hesper must have reeled against the low oak foot-post of the bed as she fell.

I entered the room, nerving myself for what I might see, but the room was empty.

Passing between the foot of the bed and the dressing-table, I set down my candle. Then my heart missed a beat and in the same moment the feeble flame of the candle flickered out.

For two beats of time I stood rigid, not daring to turn. It was not for fear of what I might see, but for fear that I might see nothing. I had entered an empty room, but as the candle flickered out, I fancied I saw in the mirror the reflection of something behind me. I waited before drawing a breath; then I turned and saw Hesper.

I want to be explicit at the expense of being tedious as to detail. First of all, the room was utterly dark, and yet I saw her as clearly as if it were broad sunlight. Yet there seemed nothing luminous in the little figure which sat on the edge of the bed looking up at me across the low oak foot. She was no dim shadow; there was no ghostly trapping about her. She was just as she had been when I last saw her living, except that her long pale hair, which she had been in the act of brushing when she died, lay tumbled about her shoulders. I recognised the cream-coloured dress with the elbow sleeves—they were the fashion twenty years ago—and the silver buckle clasping her suede belt.

My emotions and my powers of reasoning leaped out at once beyond my control. They were hounds straining at the leash, and the leash had broken. I could not truthfully say what I felt or what I thought. I stood there, looking into her eyes, which presently narrowed and gave back no hint of recognition.

'What are you doing here, please?' she asked coldly.

Her voice was low but very distinct. I should have recognised it anywhere. She used to have a funny, precise little way of enunciating her words, which sounded finnicky until you found out that it was unaffected.

When I tried to answer I stammered dreadfully.

'What are you—you—you—and what are you doing here?' I heard myself say.

'This is my room—our room. Haven't you made a mistake?'

In the midst of my awe and bewilderment I was made aware that she did not know me.

'Hesper!' I said.

She glared at me with a dignity which was heart-breaking because it was so childish.

'You had better not let Paul hear you call me that,' she said. 'I am afraid I don't know you. You have made a mistake. Will you please go?'

A dreadful sense of loneliness, of utter desolation, beset me.

'Hesper,' I cried, 'don't you know me?'

She gave me a blank stare and shook her head.

'No. No, I am afraid I do not. If you won't go I must ask Paul to speak to you. He is downstairs now. I advise you to be careful, for he is younger and stronger than you.'

At that my heart turned to lead within me, for I began to realise more than I could have put into the language of my own thought. After twenty years, as we count time, she knew nothing of the change she had undergone. For her, time had ceased, and the change seemed to have accentuated her simplicity. She seemed even more childish and innocent than on the evening when we had first kissed, with a May moon peering at us through a ragged screen of hawthorn.

'Who is—Paul?' I asked, low in my throat.

'He is my husband,' she answered, with a pride which made my heart ache. She had all the pretty dignity of a bride, and the modesty of a girl who was maid and wife. 'We were married this morning. And I am expecting Paul to come up at any moment because there are hooks and eyes at the back of my frock which I can't do up for myself, and I warned him that he would have to help me.'

I remembered how we had laughed when she told me about those hooks and eyes. One laughs for nothing when one is young and very happy.

'Can't I do them up for you?' I stammered.

'Oh, no, no, no. Thank you, but no.' She spoke very coldly and then frowned. 'How did you know my name is Hesper?'

'Because I know you.'

'But I'm quite sure you don't. I never saw you before.'

'Can't you remember?'

'Remember? Oh, there's nothing to remember.'

'Have you been waiting for Paul long?'

'No. A minute or two perhaps.'

'Don't you think I—I'm like him?'

She uttered the most heart-breaking laugh I had ever heard.

'You! Oh, excuse me; I didn't mean to be rude.'

'Then why do you laugh?'

'Because Paul is young and strong and splendid, while you'

'One gets older,' I said sadly.

'Not in the way you've got old. Paul will grow old very differently.'

And then I understood a little more, for I realised that it was not my body which she saw; and my soul was not the soul of the Paul Harford of twenty years since. Her eyes, which seemed to look through me rather than at me, were charged with a cold disdain. What I had made of myself was plainly written for her beholding. And while I pondered this fresh knowledge she began to move impatiently, swinging little suede-shod feet, I do wish Paul would come,' she murmured.

'Why?'

'There's something I want to tell him.'

'What is it?'

I saw a quiet dismay dawn in her eye. Then she shook her head,

'I don't remember. It's all gone—what I wanted to say to him. Isn't that silly? Paul always says I'm silly.'

'Perhaps I can help you, Hesper!'

'Oh, no, I shouldn't think you could. I'm sure to remember. Perhaps I've forgotten because I felt so ill just now.'

'Did you feel ill, then?'

'Yes, while I was brushing my hair. And I wanted Paul to come to me because there was something to tell him. And now I can't remember what it was.'

'Do you feel better now?' I asked, in the strangest, most quavering voice that ever I heard come from me.

'Oh, yes. Much, much better. I never felt so well. But I wish I remembered what I want to tell Paul.'

'Ah, my dear!' I breathed.

'You're sorry for me,' she said in her little quiet, childish way. 'Why?'

'Oh, Hesper, look at me.'

'i see you. You are not at all a nice old man. And you thought you were like Paul! Yet you are sorry for me. Why are you sorry?'

'I want to help you. Perhaps, after all, I can. When you felt ill just now you thought there was a change coming over you?'

'Yes.'

'And—and you wanted to tell him that it wouldn't make any difference, and that you'd never stop loving him.'

Her eyes brightened immediately.

'Yes, that was it. I remember now. How strange that you should know.'

'Ah, my dear, my dear! He does not need to be told, but he is the happier for being told. Hesper, don't you know me, dear?'

She bent upon me such a puzzled little gaze.

'You begin to look a little like Paul. But you are not Paul. I—I don't understand . . .'

And then I knew that she could not read my thoughts, but rather she could see the play of them. And mingled with my wild yearning to be recognised came a great thankfulness in the certain knowledge that death was not the end of all things, but a trysting-place, where yet she might meet and know and love me. And, God willing, there was time yet to change my way of life, so that this poor, deformed, neglected soul of mine might be known by her in the end. In that moment I seemed to make a score of resolutions. There were many pages of folly and dissipation to be turned, and I resolved to turn them.

'Oh, my dear, my dear,' I whispered, 'go to sleep. Paul knows that you love him as—he—loves you. Rest in peace, my dear, dear child.'

For a moment her head drooped contentedly.

'I'm so tired!' she whispered. Then she raised her head, and I saw in her eyes a new and wonderful light which I could no more describe than I could ever forget. She started up, and the word 'Paul' was on her lips.

I sprang towards her, my arms outstretched. But it was only the empty air of the night that I drew into them. She was gone, and I called in vain to her. I stood pleading with her to come back, and although my pleading was in vain I was left with no sense of loneliness or desolation.

Instead a quiet happiness, which I had never known before, was in my heart.

Then, presently, I hid my eyes with my hands and slipped down on to my knees beside the bed.

Behind the Panels

One of my many faults is that I am prone to exaggerate. If any strange experience comes to me I feel compelled, in telling it, to add a few artistic details which are generally lacking. I know this fault, and try to break myself of it. It is therefore with a very keen pleasure that I narrate this story, for it is so complete that I have no call to invent even the most trifling incident—or so it seems to me. Let me begin at the beginning, and try to omit nothing or add anything to the adventure.

It really began, I suppose, when Charles floundered into the sitting-room of my Chelsea flat one night, flung himself astride a chair, and behaved childishly.

'It's a great place,' he said, 'I've just been down. And you've got to come.'

'You've been down to Penwithic?' I asked, rather surprised.

'Went down yesterday, stopped over the night, and came back today. Phew, but I'm fagged. Five hundred miles in the train in two days is too much for me. Got a drink?'

I gave him one.

'And the manor-house is all that you hoped?' I asked.

'More. No excuse for you to back out, Eric. Simply no excuse.'

I did not want to 'back out'—I had never wanted to. When a casual suggestion had been thrown out that I should accompany Charles and his mother and sister on their summer holiday I felt myself half way up to the gates of heaven. But I did not accept too quickly or too eagerly. The truth was that Charles's sister Muriel was the best girl that ever trod the earth, and I was very shy of letting other people know that I had found it out—at least, at that time. It was my great secret. Thus, whenever Charles's mother invited me to dinner, I was almost rude in the off-handed manner in which I promised to come; and when they asked me to accompany them on this summer trip, I must have behaved at first as if they had offered me some personal affront.

There! I have exaggerated again, but I hope I have managed to make my meaning clear. I did not know at the time that my secret was everybody's knowledge—that it was even the subject of a wager between an affianced couple who were friends of mine.

'It's quite true,' Charles went on enthusiastically. 'There are salmon there, and peel, and a few charr, and heaps of trout, of course. And nearly half a mile of the fishing belongs to us if we take the house.'

'What's the house like?' I asked.

'Top-hole. Abso-bally-lutely top-hole. A little old, rambling Tudor manor-house, full of long passages and queer-shaped rooms and all kinds of odd corners. Nothing much to look at from the outside, but all right in. Not red-brick, you know, but lime-washed stone. They don't seem to have used bricks in that part of the world at any period. Oh, and two or three of the rooms are panelled in oak. Does that tempt you, dear heart?'

'It certainly does.'

'And the rent—furnished—is four guineas a week.'

I sat up sharply and stared at him.

'Four guineas a week—and half a mile of salmon fishing!'

'I know! But it's not so wonderful really. It's the only bit of preserved fishing on the river. Right up above, as far as Polcarrick, anybody can fish the river for the price of a salmon licence, which is fifteen bob for the season.'

'But even then, there's the house and furniture.'

'Yes, but it's not such a huge house, and the furniture's nothing to write home about, and the place is so beastly out of the way. The man who owns it is out in India, and I expect his agent is very glad to let it for him for almost anything.'

'It ought to have a ghost,' I remarked.

'Perhaps it has. It ought to be damp, and I daresay it is. The drains ought to be wrong, and I expect they are. We all ought to be ill, and it's even chances we shall be. But we're only going to be there a month, so cheer up. I think I will have another whisky, Eric. No, I am not on the downward path. This is a genuine case of thirst.'

Penwithic marks the end of the tidal waters of the St Fay River. Below the town bridge, where there is a lock, there is sometimes a waste of mud and sometimes deep water. Above, a merry little stream comes tumbling down the valley all the way from Brown Willy. The water above the lock is rarely brackish, although sometimes the angler who fishes with a worm—a custom permitted locally—will pull out flounders as well as trout.

On either side the river the hills rise up dark and green, their tops cutting the sky in firmly drawn lines; and in a pocket of the hillside stands the old manor-house of Penwithic, looking in the distance like a little white bird in a green nest. It makes an effective picture on a clear day, when the smoke of its chimneys floats up in a bluish grey stream against that background of trees and tangled shrubbery. There is very little garden; but its pasturage— which the agent called a park—falls in gentle slopes to the river bank.

We arrived at Penwithic shortly after five o'clock by the 'Cornish Riviera' express, and walked up to the house which is scarcely a mile from the station, all in good spirits. Although Charles had told us that the house was not much to look at from the outside we fell in love with it even from that point of view; but inside we rambled from room to room exclaiming and laughing in a kind of ecstasy.

It was indeed the sort of house to turn the heads of town-bred people. The ceilings were all so low that Charles and I were soon suffering from half a score of bumps, the passages were long and full of unexpected steps, the windows were deep set and the panes heavily leaded, and the dining-room was so perfect that Mrs Wilmer said we should be tempted to have meals all day long.

It was a very long, low room panelled in dark oak, and the furniture was properly sparse and contained no anachronisms. The fireplace was beautifully carved, and set in the middle was a painted shield of arms with many quarterings now almost effaced by the wear and tear of many years.

'Some good family lived here,' Muriel said.

'People named Trewithin,' announced her brother. 'Look, the name is up over the top. I heard they'd all died out.'

There was, as we knew, a panelled room upstairs, which Muriel had provisionally 'bagged'. We found that it was exactly over the dining-room, and of a most curious shape. As we went in the wall at our left hand went out at right angles, and then sloped away, so that the far corner formed what is geometrically known as an acute angle. Half way down this side of the room was the fireplace, also carved in oak, and immediately fronting it was the bed, an old four-poster with a canopy.

Over this room too we went into raptures, and I openly envied Muriel, who stood by the door, suddenly quiet.

'You can have it if you like,' she murmured. 'I don't want it '

Of course I would hear of no such thing.

'But I don't want it really,' she insisted. 'I don't like it somehow. I won't sleep here, so have it if you want it.'

Just then I heard Mrs Wilmer give vent to a little suppressed scream, and hurried to her side. She was standing before the hearth, examining the carving above the grate.

'What a dreadful face!' she exclaimed.

She had said no more than the truth. Dreadful, if anything, was too mild a word. A carved head protruded from the woodwork, with the most devilish-looking face it were possible to conceive. In my worst dreams I had never imagined anything like it.

Even Charles, who had come up, shuddered while he laughed.

'One of the Trewithins,' he said. 'They must have been a handsome family. No wonder Muriel doesn't want to sleep here.'

But Muriel had not seen that horror, and what was more, refused to look at it.

'What's the matter, Muriel?' her mother asked. 'Has the journey been too much for you?'

'I feel depressed,' Muriel announced in a matter-of-fact voice, and accompanying the statement with a smile. 'I expect it is the journey.'

Just then Charles became excited.

'Wait a moment,' he cried, and dashed out of the room, blundering into the next one down the passage.

In less than a minute he returned.

'Just as I thought,' he cried. 'The wall of the next room is quite straight. There is a huge space in the shape of a triangle between the two walls. Therefore there is a secret room in between.

'And here,' said Mrs Wilmer, advancing to the panels, 'is the secret door.'

There, to be sure, it was; but it was a poor attempt at secrecy. Nobody who searched for it could fail to find it. Indeed, it was hinged. The only thing to distinguish it from a cupboard was that it had no handle. I went to it and forced in open with my nails.

A disappointment was there to receive us. The interior was bricked up, and all we had to gaze upon was a block of masonry.

'That's funny,' said Charles, i wonder why they bricked it up. And what a rotten secret-hiding place to have, anyway. Why, even if the shape of the room hadn't given it away, nobody could help noticing the door. But there must be a tremendous hollow space behind those panels.

We went downstairs and ate an early supper. Over the meal Muriel's depression seemed to lift a little, and the rest of us waxed merrier than ever. We had our coffee served to us in the garden, and while we drank it, Charles and I argued fiercely as to which of us should sleep in the panelled bedroom. In the end we compromised by agreeing to take it in turns, and the spin of a coin decided that Charles should have it for the first week.

Looking back on the days that followed immediately after that, they seem almost perfect through the rose glasses of my memory. I refer to just the first three or four. Afterwards— but I shall come to those latter days in due time. We almost lived out of doors, despite the attractions of the house.

Sometimes Charles and I fished, and Mrs Wilmer and Muriel looked on. I may here state that we went home without catching any salmon or peel or charr, but we landed plenty of trout between eight and twenty-four ounces, and these gave us all the fun we needed.

During that time I plotted and contrived to get Muriel to myself. This was not easy, for Muriel gave me little help, and Charles liked my society and saw that he got it. Once or twice I caught myself thinking seriously what a bad son he must be to give his mother so little of his attention! But there were a few happy occasions when we walked and talked undisturbed; and on one of these she opened her mind to me.

I ought here to state that, seeing her through the eyes of love, and covertly watching her every movement and change of expression, I could see that she was not happy. She made pretences that deceived even her mother and brother, but not me. One evening, when I had her to myself for a few minutes, I asked her point-blank what was the matter.

She raised her eyes slowly and regarded me with a half-smile, 'I hoped you wouldn't notice,' she said. 'I didn't want to spoil things for you and Charles and mother. No, I'm not a bit happy, and I shan't be while we're in this house.'

'But why?' I demanded. 'What's the matter with it?'

'I don't mind telling you,' she said, after a short hesitation. 'Mother and Charles would only laugh, but I don't think you would.'

'Of course I wouldn't,' I said: you may guess at the inflection of my voice.

'I had the feeling first of all on the evening we arrived, when we were exploring Charles's bedroom. I felt awful. And I've had that feeling ever since, although not quite so badly. I'm sure this is a bad house—a dreadful house.'

'In what way?' I asked.

'I don't know. It's just something that I can feel. I am quite sure that something hellish has happened here.'

The way that word hellish slipped off her tongue gave me a little thrill.

Somehow she seemed to have hit upon its real meaning, although she did not speak with undue emphasis.

'And it happened,' she added, 'in that panelled bedroom.'

I stared at her blankly, and she returned my look with a heavy gravity which presently lightened, and her lips lengthened into a smile. For the first time in her life she gave me some little token of endearment, picking up my hand and giving it a gentle squeeze.

'Don't tell the others, that's a good boy,' she said; and I went off to puzzle over what she had said about the house, and to wonder if she had meant to be anything more than kind when she had given me that little grip of the hand. Youth, forever making mountains out of mole hills, sets great store on such things.

Of course, we had been making jokes about ghosts ever since we had entered the house, but until that night nobody except Muriel showed the least symptoms of nerves. That night, however, was the beginning of a restless time which began with small happenings and worked its way to a climax.

Mrs Wilmer, going up to dress, heard somebody walking in front of her; and I, while I was shaving in my room, had that uncomfortable feeling of not being alone, with which most people are familiar. The two maids whom the Wilmers had brought with them were scared without knowing why; and after dinner, while we were playing bridge in the drawing-room, we distinctly heard footfalls in the room overhead, when at the time both maids were in the kitchen.

I have heard of hundreds of experiences similar to those we endured during the next few days. Something was in the house with us, something neither good nor clean, something that we could feel and hear but not see. And during those days our nerves went all to pieces.

The house was haunted, even as Muriel had suggested—and badly haunted. If one of us entered a room in the twilight something invisible would get up out of a chair and pass us. We could hear the chair creak, and the stealthy sound of invisible feet creeping over the carpet. Some dreadful restless presence lingered in the dark passages and went before us or shuffled close on our heels. At different times we all experienced the disquieting sensation of having somebody peering over our shoulders.

I asked Charles if he had seen or heard anything in his bedroom, and he looked at me queerly.

'You've got to sleep there soon,' he said, 'and I'd sooner you did it with an open mind. We can compare notes afterwards. But if you think your nerves are likely to give way, for Heaven's sake sleep somewhere else. There are plenty of other rooms, and there's no need'

But I cut him short, and would not hear of foregoing my turn.

I do not pretend that I was anxious to sleep in that particular room, or that I would not have been glad of some other excuse for not doing so. But I was anxious not to appear in a poor light with Muriel in the house, and I comforted myself with the reflection that if Charles had endured it, whatever happened in that room could not overtax my own resources of courage. I had known Charles a long while, and in any emergency I should have been willing to back my nerves against his.

'That's good,' he said, 'if you'd have jibbed, mother and Muriel would want to know why, and they're quite jumpy enough as it is.'

He looked away into the distance, and his mouth spread in a mirthless smile.

'Damned cheap house, this, at four guineas a week,' he said. 'Not damp, drains in perfect order, half a mile of good fishing; and of course it can't be haunted, for there aren't such things as ghosts, as any sensible person 'ud tell you. We'll compare experiences after you've had a night there.'

And so we did. After breakfast on that particular morning we took our pipes out on to the sunny lawn, and walked up and down talking in low voices.

'Well?' said Charles.

'Well?' I said; and we looked at each other.

He glanced at me curiously out of the tail of his eye.

'Hear anything?'

'Yes. I heard it behind the panels over by the fireplace. A noise like somebody beating the woodwork with their fists; and tearing at it with their nails. It was beastly. It was such a—such a horrible frenzied sound as if somebody had gone mad in there. '

'Rats,' said Charles, 'any sensible person would tell you it was only rats.'

'Don't fool, Charles,' I begged, it was too damned awful.'

'I know. I've had some! What did you see?'

'I saw—him!' I whispered.

'Ah!'

'He was standing between me and the window when I woke up. I thought for a moment it might be you. Then I knew it wasn't—and I sweated horribly. He stood still at first, and then he moved about the room quite aimlessly for five or six minutes. I watched him with one eye open, and lay quite still. Charles I—I pretended to be asleep. I was afraid if he knew I was awake that he might want to talk to me or touch me, and I couldn't have stood that.'

'Just what I did,' Charles confessed.

'And his face! My God! It was worse than the carved face over the hearth. Not the same face, but rather like it—and worse. And there was a faint smell that was almost worse than all. It was very faint, but—ugh! Like something burning.'

Charles nodded.

'I know! Like something stale and rotten that has got into a bonfire. Did you see him clearly? I mean, did he look solid?'

'Oh, yes.'

'The first time I saw him he was less than a shadow. I could see the window curtains through him, but every night after that he got more and more solid. Things are working up towards something. I daresay he attains his greatest power on some special night of each month—perhaps at the full moon. The moon's nearly at the full now.'

'Charles, who is he?'

He shrugged his shoulders.

'How can I say? One of the Trewithins, I suppose. You can see the likeness to his face in that carving over the grate. They must have been a nice family. I say, don't give up the room. It's too interesting.'

'It's much too interesting for me! Look here, Charles, I don't care what you think of me, but I'd sooner die than pass another night alone in that room.'

'You can't complain much of loneliness,' he remarked grimly, it's all right, old chap; I know you're catching it worse than I did. I'll come and turn in with you.

'But won't that make your mater and Muriel think'

'They won't know. I'll undress in my own room, rumple up the bed-clothes, and then come in to you. It'll be all right when we're together.'

And so we settled it.

For two nights we lay side by side watching and whispering. We heard that frenzied tearing and beating at the panels, and we saw that awful phantom that grew suddenly out of the dusk and wandered around the room.

There was something dreadfully suggestive in the way he paced up and down. I had seen people suffering violent pain walking a room in just the same manner. And his fingers were hooked in agony like the claws of a bird.

When he was there Charles and I caught each other by the hand like children, and we could hear both our hearts racing like mad machinery. The second morning after we had slept there together, Charles, who had gone back to his own room to dress, came in again and found me drying myself after my bath.

'I've got a theory about this space between the panels,' he said. 'The wall is very thick underneath between the dining-room and the morning-room. There's a stair-case leads down from this room under the house.

'Stale,' I answered, 'I've thought of that.'

'Wait a minute, though! You haven't thought of this. There must be an underground passage leading down to the river somewhere. Nearly everybody in the good old times did a bit of free-trade in this part of the world, and the tidal waters used to come up here before the lock was put up. Therefore it was perfectly possible to run cargoes up as far as this.'

'Well?'

'Well, this secret door, which gives itself away at first sight, isn't the entrance to the passage at all. It is only a blind. Suppose the preventitive men searched the house they would see at once that there was a huge space between the walls. "Oh, yes," the owner of the house would say, "there was a secret passage, but we have had it bricked up." And he would open that obvious door and show the great mass of masonry inside. Whereas all the time the door is further down the panels—the real door!'

'That's an idea,' I said. 'Let's hunt for it.'

But we could find nothing, and gave up the search after a few minutes; but Charles still maintained his theory.

The night that followed was the worst of all. I pray Heaven I may never spend another like it!

Charles and I went out for a long tramp that afternoon, walking to St Fay and back along by the wooded banks of the river. We were back late and missed dinner, and the meal we managed to snatch was not a satisfactory one. When we were in bed we both discovered that we were still very hungry. It led to Charles making a suggestion.

'It wouldn't be a bad idea to have another meal,' he said. 'Shall I go down and see what I can find?'

'All right,' I said.

'And we'll have the whisky up,' he added, i don't suppose there'll be much—some cake or something. I believe they eat pasties in the kitchen, and I'll see if there are any left.'

As he spoke he clambered out of bed, thrust his feet into a pair of bedroom slippers, and put on his dressing-gown. As he was about to leave the room he turned.

'Shall I leave the candle alight?' he asked.

'No, it's all right,' I assured him.

Afterwards Charles informed me that he was not absent from the room for more than five minutes, and if that be so, the thing that I am about to relate must have happened in an incredibly short space of time, for some minutes had already elapsed when I had that dreadful feeling of not being alone in the room.

I was not nervous at being left by myself. Human society is of such value that it seems almost to negative the powers of darkness; and although Charles was not with me he had been absent only so short a while, and would be returning so very soon, that I was not in the least uncomfortable until I felt that presence.

A few moments later I saw him. He drew out of the dusk in his old place between me and the window. There was little light in the room, but he, my visitant, showed up with an appalling clarity, as if, like the moon and the stars, he diffused light of himself. It was a pale greenish light as sickening as the faint smell that now pervaded the room.

Never before had I seen this thing looking so little like a spirit. He looked to have weight, to occupy space. And yet I cannot say how he was dressed, nor could Charles who also saw him before that vile scene was ended. I kept trying to tell myself that he could not hurt me—that this thing let loose from hell had no power, except for fear, over living flesh and blood. But still my heart hammered and my flesh recoiled from this unclean presence, and I prayed in vain that I might faint.

Suddenly he crossed the room to my bedside in two or three rapid noiseless strides. Horrible as this was it seemed to free me of the paralysis that had at first taken hold of my limbs, for I leaped out of bed on the other side and shrank against the wall. I stared at him thus, my back propped up against the- oak panels, my hands flung wide and gripping their edges for support.

A shaft of moonlight striking in through a chink of the blind shone on naked steel. He had a sword in his hand, a long, shining sword. One moment and he stabbed the bedclothes, grunting with the vigour of the blow. Half a dozen times he trust at the spot where I had lain, and I heard the bedclothes being thrashed by limbs flung to and fro in agony, and as I gazed sick almost to death with the horror of it, I saw a huddled shape lying where I had lain. Then my head seemed to grow large. I had a feeling as if I were about to lose consciousness under gas. The floor seemed to heave and roll beneath my feet, and I sank slowly down into a heap, the wall at my back breaking the fall. But even then consciousness still clung to me.

There was a hideous crash on the floor, while the echoes of my own fall were yet ringing. He was dragging something out of bed, something that writhed and twisted horribly; with his left hand he dragged it out into the middle of the room, and I heard the drip, drip, drip of blood from the sodden bedclothes. And just then Charles re-entered the room.

He had set a tray down outside the door, and bore only a lighted candle. In the yellowish light the two figures in the middle of the floor grew dim, but the candle went out promptly and very faintly and distantly I heard Charles's little smothered cry of horror.

We saw the slayer and his victim reach the panels beside the fireplace, and then they seemed to die out like flames in the wind.

My next memory is of being helped out of the room by Charles, who was sobbing like a child for sheer horror.

We left the house next day and went into a farm. I had a nervous breakdown, and for three weeks I was nearer to being insane than I care to think of.

During that time the horror that I had passed through was not discussed, although Charles made a strange discovery in the manor house before we left the neighbourhood.

One afternoon he visited the panelled bedroom to make another effort to discover the outer door—the real door leading to what he believed would prove to be a secret staircase and passage. The house still being his, he had the keys and the right to come and go as he desired.

He spent two hours in steady searching, and at the end of that time met with his reward.

The innermost part of one of the panels allowed itself to be pushed upwards, leaving a space big enough to admit a human hand. Charles slipped his hand through, and his fingers encountered a knob on the inside. He turned it, and immediately the wall creaked and groaned, and a number of panels, forming an irregular door, opened out on concealed hinges.

Inside he found a narrow flight of rough steps leading down through the house inside the thick walls, and half-way down them a skeleton clad in some old rags of a nightshirt.

He exerted his courage and passed these bones, to come out eventually in a kind of cellar, from which a tunnel in the rocky soil led westward towards the river. The tunnel was, however, blocked up by a fall of rock a few yards beyond the entrance, so that he never learned where it came out.

So much for his discovery, which tallies perfectly with a legend of the house he learned from the farmer under whose roof we lived during the rest of our stay.

It seemed that somewhere back in the mists of antiquity one of the Trewithins was supposed to have murdered his brother and flung him, then half dead, down a secret staircase.

This Trewithin, like most of his family and nearly all Cornishmen, was a smuggler, and the secret passage and staircase facilitated his trade. The story went on to add that the murdered brother had been on the point of betraying the secret to the excise authorities, and that the other, becoming aware of his intention, thus took steps to prevent him.

However that may be, it fits in perfectly with that dreadful re-enactment that so nearly sent me mad, and with the blows and scratchings Charles and I both heard on the panels.

We saw that the skeleton had a decent burial, and whether or not the room be still haunted I should not like to say.

That is all. I was ill a long while, but Muriel and her mother nursed me very carefully. As for Muriel and me—but you have already guessed; and besides, this is a ghost story, and if you would have love scenes you must look elsewhere.

The Black Diamond Tree

The kindly thought must have occurred to him when he was only a few yards behind me, for, although he pulled up very swiftly and smoothly, he was a few yards in front before the car, a new and expensive one, was still. He leaned out, smiled, and waited for me to draw level with him, and I knew that he was going to offer me a ride.

'You going Kerstham way?' he asked. 'If so, I can give you a lift.'

Kerstham was my intended destination, and the last mile-stone had told me it was four miles distant. I had been walking swiftly, swinging an attaché case, with the air of a man who has a destination, and there was obviously nothing much between me and Kerstham.

I trotted up and had a foot on the running-board behind the already opened door, uttered my conventional words of thanks, and climbed in beside the Good Samaritan.

This Samaritan was a very young man; or seemed so, because we all regard men ten years younger than ourselves as very young. He might have been twenty-seven. He was tall and thin and pale, but there was nothing suggestive of weakness about his pallor. His features had that neatness of cut which Victorian ladies would have described as 'aristocratic' and there was an air of restrained melancholy about him as if he had lately suffered a bereavement. But there were no signs of mourning about his light brown plus fours, topped by a collar and tie of almost the same shade.

'Not at all,' he said pleasantly, in answer to my thanks. 'I'm glad to have company. I hope you weren't walking for pleasure or exercise and were too polite to say so.'

'I hate walking,' I assured him. 'Motoring's cured all the affection I ever had for it. But this evening there was nothing else to do. Car conked out just outside that hole of a village a mile back, and the garage people said they couldn't do anything until tomorrow. I suppose there's a decent hotel in Kerstham?'

'There are two or three of sorts, but I don't know what they're like. Glad if I've been able to be of use to you.'

While he drove fairly fast with an assumed air of carelessness we tried to make conversation. I forget what we talked about, but it was the usual pleasant trivial stuff which passes between strangers compelled to pass a few minutes together. Suddenly, after a little lull in our talk, he turned to me and said very unexpectedly: 'Unless you particularly want to go to an hotel, why not let me put you up for the night?'

Since I didn't know the man from Adam it was an embarrassing invitation.

I began to stammer that I couldn't dream of imposing myself on him.

'You will be doing me a kindness,' he said simply, as if he meant it. 'I have very few visitors.'

'And I've only some pyjamas and a toothbrush with me,' I said.

'That's all you need. You'll see nobody but the servants and myself.'

What could I say without affronting him? But I accepted against my better judgment. Why was this young man, attractive enough in his personality, obviously well born and well educated, seemingly friendless and living alone with a staff of servants? It wasn't in the ordinary nature of things. There was another pause, so I said briskly:

'Well, in the circumstances perhaps I had better introduce myself. My name's Digby.'

'Mine's Harboys.'

'Let me see,' I said thoughtfully, 'haven't I heard of a Sir Charles Harboys?'

'That's my name, but I expect you mean my father. He died two or three years ago.'

Yes, it must have been the father of whom I had heard; but what I had heard of him was gone from my mind. Somehow though, I was aware that it was nothing pleasant.

We entered Kerstham, and Harboys turned to me and said: 'Do you mind if we stop for a minute. I've got a call to make.'

He pulled up before the old archway of the Chequers.

'Got a bill to pay,' he explained, i get my wines and spirits through the people here. I dare say you'd like a drink. If so, there's a comfortable smoke-room and I shall not keep you long.'

I thought his suggestion a good one. And in the smoke-room there occurred one of those unexpected meetings which are forever taking place in country hotels. There were two men in the room when I entered, both in flannels and evidently hot from tennis, and drinking beer with gusto out of plated tankards. One of them I used to know well, but I had not seen him for years.

'Hullo, Hencham!' I exclaimed. 'Fancy seeing you here!'

'Not so odd, seeing that I live in this part of the world. But what are you doing?'

'Oh, I'm passing through. Car conked out, so I've got to spend the night here.'

'What, here? In this hotel?'

'No, I'm staying with a man named Harboys.'

Hencham looked startled. 'What, that fellow! Do you know him?'

'I haven't yet been to his place,' I parried. 'What sort of a house is it? Interesting?'

He uttered a little dry laugh.

'Interesting Too damned interesting, I should think!'

Of course, I wanted to fish for information, but before I could say more than a word or two, Harboys was in the room. He and Hencham exchanged the briefest nods.

'I'm ready when you are,' Harboys said to me, 'but I don't want to hurry you.'

That I could see was untrue. He did want to hurry me, and I could see it.

Obviously he and Hencham were not friends. I hadn't even had the drink for which I came, but I went out with him at once and followed him into the car. Just then I would have given anything to get out of my night's engagement. The approach to Dendring Court was delightful. Harboys turned the car through the open gates beside a lodge into a long straight avenue of elm and oak, with part of the facade of the house visible at the end of the long vista. The outside of the house was impressive but not particularly beautiful. It was old enough—early Jacobean, I should think, or perhaps even earlier—but too many subsequent owners had indulged their respective tastes in architecture. The gardens were beautifully kept.

I had expected to find the grounds a wilderness and the house a ruin.

Hermits, however wealthy, generally prefer to surround themselves with squalor.

Nor could the neatest housewife, nor connoisseurs of old furniture, pictures and china, have uttered a word of reproach against the interior. My host took me straight to the gun-room.

'You'd better have that drink now,' he said grinning. 'I see you know Hencham?'

'Yes,' I said.

'Ah,' he remarked, 'we're not very good friends.'

A model butler appeared in answer to a bell lightly touched, and reappeared with a tray on which were glasses and a syphon. While I drank the whisky and soda Harboys had mixed for me I noticed on the mantelpiece the photograph of a girl. She was quite pretty, I thought, but in no way remarkable, and the photograph would have left no impression on my mind if I hadn't seen portraits of her in nearly all the downstairs rooms.

'Perhaps you'd like to see over the house?' Harboys suggested presently.

'You may find it rather interesting. Dinner won't be for another hour.'

Of course, I put myself in his hands, and it was on this tour of inspection that I noticed the several likenesses of the girl whose photograph I had seen in the gun-room. Had we here, I wondered, a romantic young idiot who, having been jilted, posed as being heart-broken, and was aping the romantics of an early school of fiction by living as a solitary?

That didn't account for Hencham's words and tone; nor would a man who had sent himself 'to Coventry' seek the company of a stranger. Besides, Harboys' manner, although slightly melancholy, was not that of a man attempting to advertise a 'secret sorrow'. This was no House of Usher. It was a beautifully kept country home, obviously staffed by a number of efficient servants and—as it seemed to me—wasted on a young man who was mysteriously without friends.

All the while Harboys was fairly bright, pointing out to me without any ill-bred airs of pride of possession this picture or that article of furniture. He was the normal host showing a guest over his house. At that time I saw nothing unusual or abnormal in him, and wondered the more.

I saw the first symptoms of his queerness—that is the word I prefer to use—when he took me around the gardens. The house faced east, and on the southern side were tennis courts, the grass beautifully kept but the standing nets rotting between their posts, witnesses that nobody came to play tennis with Harboys. The half acre of turf was flanked on one side by fruit trees. It was late August and large apples—I can never remember the names of the different sorts of apples—were hanging in thick clusters, ruddy or green, and seemed already ripe for picking.

But the first tree, as one crossed from the path under the wall of the house was a large old tree smothered with great plums of so deep a purple that they were almost black. They were already over-ripe, and a few belated wasps were still busy among the windfalls. The ground beneath was strewn with them, and one or two rustled and cracked their way through leaves and twigs and plopped on the ground as we approached.

'What wonderful plums,' I remarked. 'What are they called?'

'Black diamonds,' Harboys answered, with an indifference which I afterwards knew to be studied. 'I think,' he added, with the air of one making a grim joke over the head of a child, 'that they are aptly named.'

One fell at my feet as he spoke, and I picked it up with the intention of robbing the wasps.

'May I?' I asked, beginning to pull at the skin.

A curious change came over him. He seemed half frightened, half angry, wholly vehement.

'For God's sake, no!' he cried. 'Don't touch anything off that tree. Drop it! Drop it, I tell you! Don't even touch it.'

I did as he asked. With an effort he seemed to pull himself together.

'I'm sorry,' he said. 'You'll think I'm frightfully odd. But I'd rather you didn't touch any of those plums. They're—well, I don't consider them good to eat. You can have a barrow-load of the fruit if you like, but not those.'

I dropped the offending plum and tried not to look too surprised. Harboys tried to smile apologetically.

'I ought to have that infernal tree down,' he muttered. 'I'm always meaning to. But I daren't. I wonder what would happen if I did. I wonder what the old devil would do to me if I did.'

As a man who is fond of food, and knows good food when he meets it, I must say that it was an admirable dinner. We were perfectly waited on by the ideal butler and a footman with the profile of a knave of spades and the manners of an acolyte. When we were left alone with the port Harboys pushed over a box of cigarettes.

'Well,' he said, eyeing me with a kind of sly, self-deprecatory humour, 'why do you think I'm doing this—living here all by myself, with all the people of my own kind living around me hating me like an adder.'

'I didn't know ' I began awkwardly.

'Oh, but you guessed. You know Hencham, and you saw a bit of it to-night. He'll tell you all about me if you go and see him tomorrow. I don't want to embarrass you, but you may as well hear my story first. If it won't bore you'

'Carry on,' I said.

'Well, in the first place there was a pretty useful scandal about me, which I didn't deserve. In the second place I'm mad.'

I took a sip at my port without, I hope, too evident an air of nervousness, it's all right,' he laughed, 'I'm not violent, and if I were you could cope with me. And I can assure you that my insanity doesn't take a form which is unpleasant to anybody but myself. Forgive my egotism. I meet so few people that I can talk to. May I tell you all about it or will it bore you stiff?' it certainly won't bore me,' I promised.

'Thanks. Then I'll put it into very few words. You seem to have heard of my father—or me— for I was cursed with his name. He was a popular man, hard-riding, hospitable, absurdly generous on public platforms, and loved by everybody who hadn't too much to do with him. In his own home and among his servants he was an unspeakable brute. He bullied my mother to death—sneered her to death. He hated me for not being like himself. He wanted for a son something brutal and brainless, the vicious, old-fashioned squire. By some freak of nature he begot something that grew up sensitive and, I suppose, scholarly. In return I hated him like hell.

'The people around here will tell you about two inquests, if you trouble to ask. The first they'll hardly remember much about. It was kept decently quiet. That was on old Stacks, our butler, who had been in the family service for forty years. He was expected to be pensioned off. In one of his charming fits of temper my father suddenly sacked him. We all loved old Stacks. Too old to get another job, and too proud to blackmail my father by airing his grievance, the poor old man committed suicide. It was a nice, quiet, friendly sort of inquest. The coroner happened to be my father's lawyer, and he sat without a jury. No awkward questions were asked. Verdict—Suicide While of Unsound Mind.

'That finished me with my father. We had the devil's own row. He loved power, and he'd brought me up to be entirely dependent on him. I have no profession, and he could have made me a pauper. There is no entail on the property and he could have disinherited me, but he thought of a richer revenge than that. A few months later, believing himself to be suffering from an incurable disease, he followed the example of old Stacks.

'But this time there was no hushed-up inquest. My father had written a letter to the coroner, explaining that he had taken this step because of my ingratitude and the general wickedness of my life. I had to go into the witness-box, and I didn't cut up at all well. The medical evidence revealed to me that my father was a hypochondriac, and convinced the coroner and jury that I was a liar, besides being a scoundrel and an ungrateful son. My father was popular in the county, remember, and I, not much more than a boy, who had not my father's gift for making friends, publicly branded as his moral murderer and a man to be shunned by decent people.'

'I should have thought,' I said, 'that you could have lived that down.'

'Yes,' he agreed moodily, 'i suppose I might have lived it down, but for one other circumstance. One person stuck to me, in the teeth of her parents' wishes, and that was the girl to whom I was engaged. I have several photographs of her about the place. Perhaps you have noticed . . . ?'

I nodded.

'Are you still engaged?' I ventured to ask.

'No, I broke it off. When I discovered that I had gone mad what else could I do? Unfortunately I told the facts to Rosa's people—who didn't love me much. Very soon the countryside heard that I had jilted Rosa and owned to being off my head. That put the complete tin hat on me. People can tolerate a pretty bad hat, but not a bad hat who is also a lunatic. That's why you find me living like this. Nobody of my own set, except one or two friends who live at a distance, dreams of coming near me. Well, that's my story. Imagine how glad I am of your company if only for one evening.'

'It's pretty tragic,' I agreed. 'Why don't you clear out? Travel. Do anything.'

'I can't. Under the terms of the will I have to be in residence for eleven months in the year, else the estate passes to a cousin. My father had thought of all that. I have no profession, and if I chucked it I should be a beggar. Besides, any man with any backbone ought to stay on and fight the whole thing out.'

'I wish I could help you,' I said, it is rather odd that you should tell me you are mad. Most people who are really mad don't know it.'

'Then I can assure you,' he answered dryly, 'that I am one of the exceptions.'

'If you really are,' I said, 'I think I can tell you what form it takes. Persecution mania. You think the whole world's against you.'

'In other words I am deluded about all I have just told you?'

'A good part of it, perhaps.'

He shook his head and laughed rather sadly.

'I only wish you were right. I suffer from delusions of another sort. I don't want to discuss them, though.'

'Anything to do with plums?' I asked slowly.

'Good heavens, no! Oh, I see what you're getting at. Well something perhaps to do with that tree of black diamonds.'

I was sorry for Harboys, but in no way nervous of him. When at last I went to bed I could not guess that I was about to pass the most wretched night of my life. My room was large, airy and comfortable, with two tall double windows in the wall facing my bed.

I don't know what time it was when I woke. I should think it must have been about two in the morning.

I woke up wondering where I was, as one is apt to wonder in a strange room. Then I remembered, and as I remembered I was conscious of a face bending down close over mine. It was a man's face, clean-shaven, elderly, indescribably evil and menacing, and round as the moon. It was the roundest face I ever saw. And it was yellowish and slightly luminous like the moon seen through a thin cloud. The lips were moving as if in speech, but I heard nothing.

I have no intention of trying to describe the excess of terror which froze my soul inside my body. I tried frenziedly to push the thing away from me, but there was nothing tangible about it. After a moment or two it went of its own volition.

There was no body attached to it. It floated, bobbing slightly like a child's toy balloon, and fronted me once more across the foot of my bed.

Once more those dreadful lips moved, and although there was silence in the room save for the thumping of my own heart, I had not the least doubt of what they were saying. The words were conveyed to my consciousness by some medium other than my ears.

'Go and look down at the plum tree Go and look down at the plum tree. '

I lay stiff as a board and dripping with sweat, but the Face seemed to know that I had understood, for presently it faded like a slowly expiring flame. Whole minutes must have passed before I could move. I knew what I had to do. I knew which plum tree was meant. My windows overlooked the tennis courts and the black diamond tree. I did not know what horror awaited my gaze down below, but I had to get up and look, else, I was sure, that other Horror would return and reiterate its command.

I blundered somehow across the floor, and looked out and down.

My windows were open and there was plenty of light from the stars.

Through the still night air I could hear quite clearly the creaking of one of the old plum-tree's branches. There was good cause for that creaking, for something dangled from that heavy lower limb ... a foot or two of rope, and the shape of a man swinging gently by the neck. Well, I had seen what I was told to see . . .

I dressed and paced the room for the remainder of the time of darkness, and with both the burners of electric light turned on. I shan't easily forget the slow passing of those small hours, nor how long it seemed to take the creeping dawn to grow to full daylight. I went down and out in the garden as soon as the sun was up—but not in that same garden in which the plum tree stood. After some while Harboys heard me stirring and came down to join me. The sight of my face brought him to a halt, and he uttered an involuntary ejaculation of dismay.

'You don't look well,' he said, is anything the matter?'

'I've had a most damnable nightmare or—or something,' I said, 'I thought I woke up, and there was a most filthy face bending over me, a dirty yellowish face'

'My God!' exclaimed Harboys, and his own face sprang alight with amazement and, strangely enough, something like hope. 'Nothing but a face?'

'Nothing but a face and very round and indescribably evil.'

Harboys began to tremble all over with excitement.

'I know what happened then. I know what happened. He made you go and look at the plum tree. Yes, and you needn't tell me what you saw. It's all true, then! Thank heaven it's all true. I didn't believe before. I couldn't believe. The Face you saw was my father's. The thing you saw hanging was Stacks, the butler. They both hanged themselves from that same tree. Oh, man, man, you don't know what you've done for me.'

And he came to me laughing hysterically and wrung both my hands.

'You seem pretty pleased about my having had a perfectly vile experience,' I said not very graciously.

'What of me? I see them every night.'

'I understand. And you brought me in to share the treat?'

'You don't understand!' he cried. 'Man, man, they're real. Others besides me can see them. Something can be done . . . exorcism . . . something . . .'

'I should get it done, then,' I said briefly, 'and pretty quick.'

He put his hands on my shoulders, his eyes shining.

'Oh, I'm sorry for your sake that I knowingly afflicted that foul time on you. But for my own sake I can't help being glad. I'll try to make it up to you in some way. Think what it means to me. I can go back to Rosa. I'm not mad after all.'

Dark Horses

No (said Thomley) that's by no means the queerest story I've ever heard, whether I believe it or not. It's got your tale, Bums, beaten to a rag. And I believe it.

I don't believe it necessarily because it was told to me by a parson. Even they are permitted to draw the long bow in fun. But Hendring, who told me, was dead serious. I've known him since we were boys, and he was truthful long before he ever thought of wearing a parson's collar. A fine chap is Hendring, and, odd as his story is, I'm sure that it's true.

It happened some years ago in Hendring's first parish, not long after he was ordained. He asked me, if I ever repeated it, not to mention the name of the town. It was a town of— then—twenty to thirty thousand inhabitants, within thirty or forty miles of London.

Hendring was the only curate at one of the three churches in the place. It was a difficult kind of parish to work, for the clergy hardly knew who were and who were not their parishioners.

But he hadn't a bad time there, he told me, which I suppose means that he got on well with the Vicar and found that he could live in reasonable comfort on his stipend and his own small private means.

In a town which isn't too large, a man—particularly a parson—soon gets to know a tremendous lot of people by sight. And, naturally enough, he takes particular notice of those who look a bit unusual. So he came to notice young March.

Young March was a tall, pale boy of about fourteen, who wore a black coat and glasses and was never seen to smile. A most serious and seemingly self-centred person was young March. Always he raised his hat to Hendring, who thought at first that he was home from school on holidays, and afterwards on sick-leave. He mentioned the boy to the vicar who shook his head.

'Oh, no,' he said, 'young March doesn't go to school. He has a private tutor. Odd boy. Odd people altogether.'

'Anything wrong with him?'

'N-no. Not that I know of. I don't know them at all. They're not in our parish and I've no excuse for calling.'

It wasn't, of course, Hendring's affair. But he wouldn't have been much of a parson if he hadn't been sorry to think that this rather odd boy was probably being brought up without any kind of religious education. He soon got to know plenty about the boy's environment, and while it didn't exactly satisfy him, nobody could say that it was bad.

He was orphaned of both father and mother and in the guardianship of his stepfather, a man named Wright, who had given out that the boy was too highly strung and sensitive to be happy at school and he had thus engaged a tutor for him.

Lofting was the name of the tutor. He seemed a very good sort. Nobody could say that the boy was not in good hands, and indeed it was rumoured that if he went to school he already knew enough to be put in one of the upper classes.

Nobody knew very much about Wright, except that he was reputed to be a rich man. The absence of womenfolk in the house kept away callers, but the two men were liked well enough by more or less casual acquaintances. Sometimes they visited hotel bars, where they drank with moderation and were courteous and friendly—but not too friendly—with all those with whom they came in contact.

All that could be said in criticism of them was said in the frequently uttered remark: 'Why isn't that kid at school?'

It can hardly be said that Hendring got to know the boy by accident. He meant to speak to him as soon as he had the chance. And the chance came one afternoon when Hendring's leisure allowed him to take a stroll by the river. On the landward side of the path he came upon the boy stretched out in the shade of trees. He had a writing pad before him and as Hendring approached he saw the boy smuggle something out of sight between his arm and his prostrate body. Then he grinned at Hendring and made a twitch at his back-tilted hat.

Since distant greetings had already been exchanged between them Hendring stopped and spoke. His age and calling allowed him to lead off with a joke.'

'Hello, you young rascal,' he said, 'what are you hiding away there? Catapult?'

Even as he spoke the absurdity of the accusation struck him. That was surely the last boy ever likely to own a catapult.

The answer was No—and a grin.

Hendring was smiling but firm. Small boys who suddenly hide things away are fair game for grown-up curiosity.

'Come'on,' said Hendring, still smiling, 'let me see what it is.'

As sheepishly as he might have produced a revolver the boy showed Hendring a planchette.

'Oh, lord,' said Hendring, i shouldn't play about with that thing.'

'Don't let my father know I've shown it to you.'

'I suppose he'd give you a good hiding.'

'Well, he'd be awfully cross.'

'Then, my dear boy, don't do behind his back things which you know he wouldn't'

The boy interrupted him, taking advantage of a slight pause of uncertainty.

'Oh, he knows about this. But he wouldn't like anybody else to know.'

Hendring felt suddenly cold and uncomfortable. The boy seemed to understand.

'I know you'll think it's wrong,' he said. 'But you won't tell anybody else. I'll tell you all about it if you like. It gives me winners.'

'Winners?'

'Yes. Race horses.'

'Good heavens! You don't mean to say they win!'

'Yes. Always. But I don't get them every day. I have to wait.'

Naturally, Hendring suspected that his leg was being pulled, it belonged to my mother when she was alive. Father used to laugh at it.

She never got any sense out of it. It all happened because it was on the dining-room table early one evening when there was an accident on the road almost outside.

'They brought in a man who was very badly hurt, our being the nearest house. Mother ran out for the doctor and left me alone with him. I gave him brandy and water while he lay groaning on the sofa.

'Presently he quietened down and looked up at me. He said he didn't think he was going to die through the accident, but the doctors had told him he hadn't long to live in any case. And then he looked across to the table and saw the planchette.

' "Oh," he said, "I know them things. Well, you get hold of it after I'm gone and I'll try to send you the right stuff."

'I didn't know what he meant at first, and then he told me that he was a bookmaker and he meant horses which were going to win. He said—he said I was a decent kid. When they'd taken him away I told Father and Mother, and they both laughed at the idea. And I didn't believe it either.

'Mother was taken ill and died soon after, and when she'd been dead for some time I found the planchette. I didn't say anything to Father, but I tried to make it write for me, in case there really was something in it. Something from her, I mean. But it didn't write at all for a long time.

'I kept on and on, trying at different times. And at last it began to write. I felt as if there was something inside my arm, pushing my hand along. When I looked I found I'd written: "Dolly Dear tomorrow".

'It didn't seem to make sense because I didn't know anybody named Dolly. At least not well enough to call her dear. And while I was staring at it Father came in and caught me, and I had to own up and explain. And he frowned and looked in a little green book. And then he looked at the back page of the evening paper.

'Not next morning but the morning after I saw something which I shouldn't have noticed if I hadn't remembered writing that name. "Dolly Dear's Easy Victory". And I saw my father frowning as if he was puzzled and he said something about "not much of a price, but it won all right". He asked me if I had ever heard of a filly called Dolly Dear, and I said I hadn't until I'd written down its name.

'Then he told me I could use the planchette as often as I liked, and I was to be sure and show him whatever it wrote. And so I did.

'Sometimes I'd get nothing for days, and then I'd find myself writing the name of a horse which always won next day. They weren't what Father calls big prices, but they always won. And then' (the boy added naively) 'father got much better off. So we moved into a bigger house here.'

Hendring stared, not knowing what to make of that extraordinary tale. Of course he couldn't believe it. But the boy seemed serious enough and evidently expected to be believed.

'So Mr Lofting came to be your tutor?'

'Yes. Father wouldn't let me go away to school. He says wait until he's a millionaire. He's explained it all to me. He says he daren't get too rich all at once. Even now, he says he has an awful job to place his commissions. He backs losers sometimes on purpose.'

Hendring went on listening to the incredible tale which fell so glibly from the boy's tongue.

'And does your—er—tutor back horses, too?' he asked.

'Oh, yes. You see he's a friend of Father. They're really in partnership.'

Hendring hesitated over what he had next to say. It looked a suspicious sort of question coming from a man of his cloth.

'Have you had any—er—message this afternoon?' he asked.

'Yes, sir. Just before you came up. But father told me never to—'

'I shan't back it,' Hendring interrupted, smiling quietly. 'And I shan't tell anybody else. But naturally I want to test your—er—extraordinary story.'

The boy held up the writing pad on which the planchette had rested.

Something almost illegible was scrawled.

'I can't read it,' he said, is that your ordinary hand-writing?'

'Not quite, but very like it, sir. I can read it myself. You see, the words run into one another. The pencil's on the paper the whole time. But I can read it all right. It says "Dark Angel tomorrow",

'Is there a horse called Dark Angel?'

'I suppose there must be, sir. Otherwise I wouldn't have written it. But,' the boy added rather quaintly, 'I don't take much interest in horses.'

Hendring did not take much interest either in a general sort of way. He liked to see what had won the Derby and the National and occasionally, before these races, he allowed himself to be inveigled into sweepstakes from which a large percentage of the money went to sport or charity.

'Well,' he said, i'll look out for it and see if it wins. And look here, young man.'

'Yes, sir?'

Hendring paused, tom by conflicting duties, and at the same time feeling rather an idiot. The whole thing was monstrous. Several things were quite clear, supposing the boy to have told him the truth, and it was an odd story for a boy to have on the tip of his tongue all ready to trot out.

Greatly he wanted to tell the boy that he was doing wrong, but he could hardly do so without accusing the boy's own father. Here was a situation in which he felt were needed a tack and delicacy beyond his own. To speak his mind would be to alienate the boy for ever.

'Just talk to me when we happen to meet again. I shan't ask you for any more—er— winners! By the way, do you like doing this sort of thing?'

The boy hesitated and smiled, vaguely.

'I don't mind it, but'

'Well?'

'I'd like to go away to a big school. But Father says not until he's a millionaire. He must be awfully rich already, but—but he can't put as much money on as he'd like. He has a lot of trouble as it is to get the bets taken. And it's a bit dull—keeping my hand for hours and just waiting.'

'Yes,' said Hendring, smiling, i expect so. Well, goodbye for the present. Talk to me when you meet me again.'

'Yes, rather, sir.'

The boy stood up politely and uncovered. Hendring went off thinking—and wondering. He saw his vicar that evening.

'I don't know what you'll think of this tale,' he began. The vicar heard him and smiled. He smiled with an increasing smile.

'I think it's monstrous!' he said. 'Monstrous that the Cloth should permit itself to be pulled by the leg. If the young scoundrel had pitched that story to me I'd have clouted his head.'

'I'm not sure.'

'You don't mean to say that you believe him.'

'I'm not sure,' Hendring said again. 'There are people—and plenty of them—who believe that it is possible to communicate with the spirit world. And, if that is what the boy is doing, what kind of influence is guiding him? Putting it plainly, he is being made to help his stepfather to cheat.'

'Yes, of course, that would be so if it were true. Only, you know, it isn't true. You've had your leg pulled, my young friend.'

Hendring laughed confusedly.

'Well, I suppose so,' he said, 'but look at in another way. There is that peculiar household. There is the apparently abnormal boy who uses the planchette. And there is the stepfather who is apparently a very rich man.'

'Yes, I give you all that. And then I say suppose—only suppose—it were true, what could one do about it? Absolutely nothing. The boy is being well cared for and well educated. The law could do nothing. And we should be laughed at and sneered at if we tried to set it in motion. We are told to mind our own business if we take notice of a public scandal. We are quite helpless here. But, of course, my dear fellow, it just isn't true.'

Hendring shrugged his shoulders and laughed again.

'We'll give it some sort of test,' the vicar resumed. 'He told you the name of a horse which was going to win tomorrow. Dark Angel. If there is such a horse and it wins it will prove nothing. The boy has got to hear of it from his—er—undesirable guardians. And if there is no horse of that name, or if it doesn't win, it will prove that you have—er—had a little joke played on you.'

'All right,' said Hendring. 'Heads you win, I suppose, and tails I lose.'

'We can learn a little now,' the vicar resumed, smiling. 'Here is the evening paper. It will give the names of the horses entered for tomorrow's meeting. On the front of the back page, if—er—my memory serves me. Yes, here we are. Tomorrow's Programme for Windsor. Well, well, it's a long time since I looked at this page with any interest.'

He paused and put on glasses to read the small print. There was silence for two or three minutes while he frowned over the page. Presently he handed the paper over to his curate.

'There you are, my dear fellow. I don't see that name on the list of horses engaged.'

Hendring read while the vicar quietly enjoyed his little triumph.

'No,' Hendring admitted, i don't see it here either. But perhaps it's at some small meeting—a point-to-point or something'

The vicar laughed.

'Now my dear fellow!' he exclaimed, wagging a finger. 'Be a sportsman. Even if that were so the information would be valueless to your young friend and his connections. The bookmakers do not accept commissions on these events. No, you have had your leg pulled.'

Hendring shrugged his shoulders and smiled. There was no more for him to do. He had the average man's dislike for owning himself to be wrong, and he had all the while a sneaking, and not very comfortable, suspicion that he was not wrong after all.

He went on studying the paper. Perhaps the oracle spoke in riddles. But he could not see a mention of any horse with a name suggestive of angels, or, for that matter, with demons or death. But Dark Angel was what the boy had written—or said he had written.

'I suppose,' the vicar commented with a calm smile, 'there's a lot of joy in certain quarters when a parson's leg is successfully pulled.'

'I dare say,' Hendring agreed, smiling lazily.

On the following evening they were together in the vicar's study when the evening paper arrived. The vicar took it from the maid and smiled at Hendring.

'We will just see,' he remarked, 'if your horse, which wasn't apparently entered, has broken all records by winning a race. I hope Mary isn't listening through the keyhole. She would think that we had both gone to the dogs. Red Hussar. Now could a Red Hussar be construed to mean a dark angel? No, I hardly think so. Anyhow Red Hussar didn't win. Nor did any other horse with a colourful name'.

The electric bell rang outside and the vicar looked up.

'That'll be young Thompson,' he said. 'Wants me to sign that certificate for him. Mustn't let him see me looking at the racing. Come in.'

A fair-headed young working man shuffled in, grinned respectfully at the two clergymen, looked round for somewhere to put his cap, and finally held it between his knees while he dipped a hand into his breast pocket.

'Ah, thanks, Thompson,' said the vicar, taking a paper from his hand.

He glanced down it and picked up a pen.

'Dreadful thing happened this afternoon, sir,' the visitor said.

'Yes?' said the vicar looking up.

'You know that boy at Tudworth House. March, his name'

'Yes, I know him.'

'Fell off the top of a tree in the orchard this afternoon and broke his neck.'

There was silence. Not absolute silence, for the young man could hear, grown suddenly laboured, the breathing of the two clergymen.

When they spoke, their words were enigmatic to the tow-haired caller who stood staring at them in mild surprise.

'Dark Angel!' said the vicar in a low voice.

'Dark Angel—this afternoon,' said Hendring.

Oberon Road

I am sorry to have to begin this true tale by breaking one of the written laws of the short story. My numerous Guides to Young Authors, compiled by gentlemen of great but undiscovered literary ability, assure me that I should begin with a striking incident or some pregnant dialogue, and never—no, never—with a long and prosy character sketch.

Well, no doubt they are right, but they were never set the task of writing this particular story. If you don't like my way of doing it, you had best say au revoir, and turn over a few pages, and perhaps we may meet again more auspiciously a month or so hence. For, honestly, I don't know how to begin this tale about Michael Cubitt without telling you all that ought essentially to be known about the man.

Michael Cubitt—you who are still reading—was a man of forty-two, or maybe forty-three, and he lived in the very worst suburb in the south-east of London. He lived there for two reasons—because he had settled there as a mere boy and hated changes, and because it was cheaper than most other suburbs. For he was very fond of money, and it would seem that his affection was reciprocated, since he had plenty. Not fond of money for money's sake, mind you, but because he wanted to make sure when he grew old of having a fire by which to warm his thin hands. He had already made sure of that fire; his money was safely and skilfully invested; but good and bad habits are alike tenacious.

Cubitt was a lawyer, a partner in a City firm with an enormous practice. He had begun in the same firm as a clerk, and had prudently bought his articles with part of the one thousand pounds which Aunt Martha left him. He was thin and spare, sallow and bloodless, and his humour—what there was of it—was sardonic. He had no friends and no enemies, because so far as could be discovered, he had never done anybody a bad or a good turn.

His landlady in Fenton Road, who had been ministering to him for more than twenty years, would not have lost him for anything, but at the same time she rather disliked him. For, as she told Mrs Perkins next door, although he paid regular and gave no trouble, there was something about him that wasn't quite 'uman.

Subject to railway strikes and minor alterations in the time-table, he went up by the same train every morning, and came back by the same train every evening. His only recreations seemed to consist of reading heavy books on conveyancing, and working out chess problems which are to be found in the more intellectual kind of newspapers. He had no apparent vices and no apparent virtues. Nobody but himself knew exactly what he got out of life.

He was not even fond of fresh air, and the only exercise he took was in walking from Fenton Road to the station, and from the station back again to Fenton Road.

Fenton Road was only two or three hundred yards from the station as the crow flies, but it was actually near half a mile by road, by reason of one having to walk round three sides of a square. The streets were old-fashioned and badly planned, and Cubitt was shocked and dismayed when he came to reckon up how much boot leather he had been compelled to waste in consequence. If you wanted to go from the station to the place of his abode, you had to cross the road, turn to the right, and walk about a furlong until you came to Norman Avenue; there you turned to the left, walked down Norman Avenue for the best part of a quarter of a mile, and turned to the left again. This brought you into Fenton Road, and Cubitt's lodgings were about two hundred yards up on the left. He hated Norman Avenue cordially, and when the weather was damp, and the road was up—as it was that Christmas time—he hated it worse than ever.

It was three or four evenings before Christmas, and the weather was wet and muggy and depressing, and the only snow to be seen was on the covers of the magazines, when Michael Cubitt departed from custom so far as to speak to a stranger. What made him do it he didn't know. He was in a bad temper because of the approaching holidays, when he wouldn't know what to do with his time, and because it was raining in streaks, and because Norman Avenue was 'up', and there would be no walking on the road, and he would be jostled by young fools who insist on walking abreast, and his eyes would be imperilled by the rib-ends of innumerable umbrellas. But, in spite of all this, he actually vouchsafed an answer when the only other occupant of his compartment laid aside an evening paper and suddenly addressed him.

'A lot of rain,' said the stranger casually.

Cubitt regarded him with a long, comprehensive glance. A queer-looking fellow, this man who sat opposite him. He was tall and thin and wore his clothes as if they grew upon him, like the fur of an animal. His mouth was long and straight, almost ludicrously like a receptacle for letters, his forehead high and narrow, and his eyes small, dark, beady, and full of meaningless laughter. But it was his ears which interested Cubitt most. These were long and large and had no lobes to them, and at the tops they were distinctly pointed. He caught himself wondering if they were the ears of a criminal; at least they were the ears of no normal person.

'Wretched weather,' Cubitt grunted.

'Oh, I like it,' said the other, grinning, it makes the toadstools grow.'

Cubitt frowned slightly over what he considered to be a pleasantry which was either feeble or beyond his understanding.

'And, of course,' he grunted, 'they've taken Norman Avenue up, and the pavements will be all over wet clay which the navvies have trodden there, and I shan't be able to move for people with shopping baskets and umbrellas. I don't know what the L.C.C. is thinking of—taking up the roads at this time of the year.'

The stranger had one eye closed as if in contemplation of something, but the other, turned upon Cubitt, grew suddenly very bright and friendly.

'You live in Judge Park?' he asked.

'Yes, Fenton Road,' said Cubitt, wondering at the same time what made him so communicative.

'Ah, I know Judge Park. I'm going there myself tonight. I've got something to give to a good policeman who gave a poor man sixpence yesterday instead of running him in for being without a home.'

'Oh!' said Cubitt shortly, not greatly interested.

'So,' added the stranger, making his eyes snap merrily, 'when you see him standing up in the rain, holding up some traffic with one hand, and beckoning other traffic forward with the other, you'll know he won't really be there at all. He'll be back in a hayfield down Shropshire way.'

It was at this point that Cubitt wished he had brought an evening paper to retire behind, for he now surmised that his companion was a lunatic; and although he did not suppose him to be dangerous, he was very glad that Judge Park was the next station.

'But why go through Norman Avenue at all?' demanded the stranger, altering his tone.

'Because it's the shortest way to Fenton Road. It's the only way unless I turn to the left outside the station, and lose a quarter of a mile, and on a night like this'

'Nonsense! There's a much shorter way. Why don't you go through Oberon Road?'

'Oberon Road? I've never heard of it.'

'Cross the road outside the station,' said the stranger glibly, 'turn to your right, and it's the first turning on your left.'

'But that's Norman Avenue.'

'No, it isn't. It's Oberon Road—a long way before you get to Norman Avenue.'

Cubitt scowled because he hated to be contradicted.

'I tell you, sir,' he said, 'that there isn't any turning on the left until you come to Norman Avenue. It's all solid houses, and I ought to know because I've gone home that way every week-day evening for the last twenty-odd years.'

'Oberon Road is there,' said the stranger, 'only you haven't noticed it.'

'But it's impossible!' Cubitt exclaimed, wondering why he was taking the trouble to argue with a madman. 'Do you mean that it runs parallel with Norman Avenue and leads into Fenton Road?'

'It leads almost anywhere, and it doesn't run parallel to any road in the world that I've ever heard of.'

Cubitt was glad that the electric train stopped just then with all the abruptness peculiar to its kind, and to see Judge Park on the station lamps, although the light of them revealed straight diagonal lines of rain. He was first out of the compartment, because he had no liking for his queer companion.

'Good night,' he grunted over his shoulder.

'Oberon Road,' returned the other. 'The first on your left before you get to Norman Avenue.'

Cubitt joined the swarm of people collecting around the barrier, showed his season ticket, and went out as usual through the booking office. He did not wait under shelter to put up his umbrella, but opened it as he hurried across the road. He hurried not only because it was wet, but because he did not want to be overtaken by the madman who had been talking to him in the train. A very queer fellow, that! Fancy trying to tell him, Michael Cubitt, about a road on the left before one came to Norman Avenue! Why, it was all one solid unbroken line of villas and blocks of flats. Certainly there ought to have been a road cut through. It was scandalous that the people of Fenton Road should be compelled to go so far out of their way to and from the station. And if there had been such a road, as if he, Cubitt, wouldn't have known of it, seeing that he had gone that way every day for twenty-odd years.

So thought Cubitt as, with head down, he hurried forward under his umbrella. But he had not gone many yards ere he was brought up sharply and his thoughts rudely scattered. The pavement before him suddenly ended, as if he had reached the entrance to a side road. The curb on his right hand made a sweep to the left, enclosing him in an arc of a circle. At his feet was a gutter down which a muddy stream was flowing, to sing and splutter in a grating on the comer. Surely, he thought with a start, this couldn't be Norman Avenue already.

He lifted his gaze and knew immediately that it was not Norman Avenue.

He knew the houses on the corners too well to be mistaken. One of them was called Hazlehurst, and the other, being a place of public entertainment, was known as the Black Swan. And here were two villas which he could have sworn had hitherto been unbroken links in a long chain. He looked up, and there, painted on a board alongside one of the villas, was Oberon Road, as plain as a pikestaff!

So it was true after all, and Cubitt stood staring, holding his open umbrella down and letting the rain fall upon his head and shoulders.

'Well, I'm damned!' said Michael Cubitt, and you must understand that it was very rarely indeed that he was guilty of such an exclamation. Well, there was Oberon Road, an undoubted fact, and inviting him to take the short cut which he had so often desired. If it ran straight, he reflected, it ought to bring him out into Fenton Road close to his lodgings. And yet he hesitated. There was something eerie about it all. How was it possible that he could have been so blind as not to see this road before? He could have sworn that it wasn't there in the morning. And how could they have made a road all in a few hours?

He looked up and down Station Road. That at least was normal.

Commonplace people were moving up and down, brushing against him as he stood there. A laden motor-bus ploughed by, spurting up liquid mud. On the other side of Station Road a youth was playing a mouth-organ, and another youth was wringing his mouth awry to do a like injustice to the King's English and a popular sentimental song. And these commonplace sights and sounds heartened Michael Cubitt. Absurd to have such vague, unquiet fancies when the world about him seemed to be as normal and as ugly as ever.

In a moment or two Cubitt made up his mind. He wheeled to the left and strode boldly up the pavement of Oberon Road.

At first Oberon Road was just like any other suburban road, except that it was unlit; and as Cubitt drew farther and farther away from the main thoroughfare the darkness grew deeper, until at last he could not see his hands which grasped the umbrella. And by and by the sounds of traffic and distant voices died away, and Cubitt walked in darkness and silence. And a great awe came upon him.

But after a little while the darkness lifted. The rain clouds above him parted, and the moon looked through, like a shining face peering between curtains. And the light grew stronger and stronger, until it was as bright sunlight, and Cubitt looked around him and uttered a little gasp of amazement and delight.

For Oberon Road was such a road as he had never seen before in any suburb or in any fair city. The houses were small, but they were a delight to the eye; some were thatched and some were gabled, after the Elizabethan style, and some were plastered and showed rough old timber; for all of them looked old. And all were set in delightful gardens of flowers and fair lawns and wooded spaces in which one knew there were little hidden arbours. And strangely enough it was not winter here, and the weather was warm and fair without being hot, as in the early days of a fine May. And Cubitt, who had never before coveted anything that was lovely for its own sake, and had been content to stay on in his dingy lodgings to save expenses, caught himself thinking: i must certainly buy a house in Oberon Road, whatever it costs.'

In the front garden of one of these houses sat a girl who was lovelier than moonlight, who rocked a cradle with her foot, and sang a love song to the strumming of a guitar which she held in her white hands. So Cubitt went up to the gate, and lifted his bowler hat, and asked her if she knew of a house for sale or to be let, or failing that, would it be possible to get lodgings? And the girl stared at him curiously, and ceased singing, and shook her head.

'I really cannot tell you,' she said, 'I should inquire at the estate office.'

'And where is that?' he asked.

'Farther along. I would gladly come and show you, but Jack may be here at any minute, and it would never do for us to be absent when he came.'

'And who is Jack?' Cubitt asked.

'He is a failure, and unsuccessful poet; and when he has money he drinks; and when he has drunk he comes here for a little while. It is wrong of him to drink, but that is all understood and forgiven because he has suffered much. And because he was once kind and generous and brave, and beautiful in mind and body, they let him come here sometimes. No, I must not on any account be absent when Jack comes.'

'I see,' said Cubitt, who did not see at all. And lifting his bowler hat to her he passed on; and almost ran into Jenkins, one of his clerks, who was hurrying past in flannels, carrying a tennis racket.

'Why, Jenkins,' he exclaimed, 'fancy seeing you here!'

'Considering I live here, sir, it's really not so strange after all. That is to say, I live here sometimes. But I mustn't stop, sir, because I am going to play tennis with the dearest girl in the world. And one day, as soon as I can afford it, we are going to get married.'

'One moment, Jenkins. I want to know if I can get a house'

'I really mustn't stop, sir. You see, I didn't expect to meet you here. And, really, I get so little time for tennis.'

It was then that Cubitt remembered that Jenkins had been lamed in the War, and was no longer able to play the game which had once been a passion with him. And he passed on, wondering, to see at a garden gate a boy with a cricket bat under his arm, and a familiar blazer hanging loose over his shoulders. He recognised the boy at once and greeted him with a shout of surprise, and the boy laughingly welcomed him, addressing him as Cupid.

Now Cupid was the name by which Cubitt had been called at school.

'If it isn't young Harvey!' Cubitt exclaimed. 'And what are you doing there with that cricket bat?'

'I am going to get some practice,' said young Harvey gravely, 'because, as you know, I am going to play for Middlesex when I grow up, and I must keep my hand in. But I never thought I should see you again, Cupid. And how funny and old and queer you look! And you do look silly with that umbrella!'

'Do you live here always, Harvey?' Cubitt asked wistfully. 'Or do you only come here sometimes?'

'Why, I live here always,' said young Harvey. And then Cubitt remembered that young Harvey had died when a boy of fourteen, and fear smote him again.

'Well,' he stammered, 'I hope you will do very well for Middlesex.'

'Yes,' said the boy gravely, 'we shall have a very good team when I begin to play. What with myself and Stoddart and Trott and J.T. Heame. And they say that new man Warner is very good. So you won't mind if I run off and get some practice, will you?'

So Cubitt watched him run away, and then, carrying his bewilderment like a load, walked on up the sunlit road between the fair houses and the fair gardens. For the moon which had first made light for him had given place to the sun, and his own shadow was the only ugly thing that he could see.

And along the road he met many, who were all very beautiful and very young, youths and young girls. For the most part they walked in pairs, and these couples had no eyes for anybody else but just each other. And Cubitt read in their eyes such love for each other that his heart smote him with a pain which he had not suffered for more than twenty years, and had not thought ever to feel again.

It seemed to him that he had not walked very far ere he came to a house which was more beautiful than all the others; and why it was more beautiful he could not say, except that it gave more delight to his eyes. It was made of old red brick, with high rectangular windows, and a great wistaria in full bloom, with branches like a vine's, almost covered the face of it. Between the gate and the front door was a broad flagged path with moss and grass growing between the stones, and dividing two green lawns, on the left of which was a sundial.

And while he stood yearning after this little place of delight the door burst open and a little girl ran down the flagged path towards him. She was fair-haired and blue-eyed, and her frock was blue to match her eyes, and she wore a little white housewifely apron. And he knew her at once for Gladys, a little girl with whom he had played at being sweethearts when he was a small boy and whom he was once firmly determined to marry when he grew up.

This Gladys burst open the gate and ran straight into his arms and kissed him laughingly and violently, with a straight pursed-up mouth, as children kiss.

'Why, Gladys,' he said, 'if I had not just decided that I must give up being surprised, I should fall dead with amazement.'

'Dead?' she repeated wonderingly. 'What is "dead"?'

'And is this your house, my dear?' he asked quickly, for her question troubled him.

'And yours, too. Don't you remember it is just the house we decided we must have after we were married? And you were to have a real gun instead of one that only fired peas? And I was to have real babies instead of dolls?'

'My house?' he repeated. 'Our house?'

'Only, of course, you can't come and live in it like that. There's a regulation against it. For something has happened to you, and you're not a nice boy with inky fingers and a bag of sweets in your pocket any more.

You're a funny old gentleman with an umbrella and a bowler hat. And you can only come here as the little boy you once were. But I know you're my Michael, all the same.'

Cubitt clasped the child to him rather wearily and began to whisper to her:

'My dear, tell me how I am to help being what I am. If this is my house it is unfair that I may not come and live in it. And how am I to be once more the boy who used to play with you in fields on which the builders have made houses since?'

'Perhaps,' said Gladys, 'you have not paid for our house. And it is only as little Michael that you can live in it. Why, all your old toys are in the attic, where they have been waiting for you all these years. And I have been wanting so much to hear you recite "Hohenlinden" again.'

'But what am I to do about it?' he asked hopelessly.

'If I were you,' she said, 'I should go and see them at the estate office.'

'Is that it, over there?' he asked.

'No. Where you are pointing now is the shed where Father Christmas keeps his sledge. You can see the reindeer grazing just beside it. He is a jolly old gentleman is Father Christmas, and often comes in to see me. No, that is the estate office—farther up the road, where I am pointing now.

'My dear,' said Cubitt, still holding her in his arms, 'I do not understand it. I do not understand anything. I only know that I, who thought I had never loved anything nor could love anything save myself, now love you better than anything else in life. I say this to you, who am an oldish man while you are still a child. And if I can win back to the boyhood which seemed to have been stolen from me while I slept, I may yet share with you the house which once we built together out of a dream.'

So said Cubitt, and she kissed him again with a little happy laugh and pursed-up mouth. Then Cubitt strode down the road to the estate office. The estate office was like any other estate office, but its surroundings invested it with a kind of beauty. Cubitt tapped at the door, and a voice bade him come in, and he entered to confront a very beautiful young man with white folded wings who sat behind a roll-top desk. And a little to his left was another young man, not so beautiful, and with smaller wings, who pored over a ledger. Now it was well that Cubitt was determined to be surprised at nothing, for truly a house agent with wings is an unusual sight; and one would more expect to see a man of that calling decorated with horns and a tail. But Cubitt swallowed his surprise, even when he heard himself addressed courteously by name.

'Good-day, Mr Cubitt, and what can I do for you?'

'I want a house,' said Cubitt slowly and distinctly.

'A house? What sort of house? We have only small houses here, for those who require great mansions do not come to Oberon Road.'

'It is a small house that I want,' said Cubitt. That one with the wisteria and the sundial in front.'

'The sundial is merely a superfluous decoration, Mr Cubitt, because here it is always noon. But do you mean the house where Gladys lives?'

'That is the house. I understand that it is my house, too.'

'Yours?' He turned sharply to his clerk. 'Look it up, please, will you?'

And the clerk turned over several pages of the ledger and presently said, 'The house was built for Mr Cubitt, but he has not paid for it.'

'There you are, you see!' said the agent severely. 'And you don't think we're going to have middle-aged men with umbrellas living in Oberon Road, do you?'

Then Cubitt, controlling his voice with difficulty, said, 'I can pay for my house. You have only to say how much. For I have a great deal of money invested in gilt-edged securities, which I could realise in an hour.'

''I do not know the price, Mr Cubitt,' said the clear, hard voice. 'But I do not think that you can pay it now.'

'But—young Harvey never had any money!'

'Oh, yes, he did. He had a great deal. He had sixpence once, his week's pocket-money. And he gave it to a woman on the road who carried a baby which was starving because she was starving. And Jenkins bought his house here with a mouthful of water which he gave to a wounded man on Paschendael, when he himself was wounded. It was his last drop of water, for none dared drink from the shell-holes; so he too paid a great price for his house, Mr Cubitt. And that girl whom you first saw here, she also paid a great price, for she gave all she had to an outcast; and that was tears, and sympathy, and a message of hope.'

'Do you mean that she gave them to the drunken poet she spoke of?' said Cubitt, with just a hint of outraged virtue in his tone, 'I wonder you have such an undesirable tenant. But perhaps he paid dearly for his villa.'

'He did, Mr Cubitt. He ruined himself to save a friend, and he was never strong enough to begin again. Some men are like that, Mr Cubitt. We do not admire drunkards; but when his brain is drugged with spirits he creeps here sometimes for little blessed half hours, and because he has paid for his house we have not the heart to turn him out.'

'Ah, the poor fellow!' said Cubitt, suddenly melting.

The agent regarded him out of kinder eyes.

'How did you get here, Mr Cubitt?' he asked; and Cubitt told him.

'This is one of Dandalon's tricks,' said the clerk curtly. 'He's always trying to be funny. It's about time you told him about it.'

'And yet,' said the agent thoughtfully, 'I do not altogether blame Dandalon. For I have just perceived symptoms in Mr Cubitt which bid me hope that we may yet do business together.'

'Ah, do you think so?' cried Cubitt, his face brightening. 'But tell me—oh, tell me—how much must I pay? Is it all that I have?'

'No,' said the agent, his voice growing very gentle, 'not all that you have; but all that you think you cannot spare. And you must give all your heart with it, and try at the same time not to think of the little house which you may be buying.'

'I will! I will!' Cubitt cried, very close to tears.

'Ah, well, then, perhaps we shall see you again not as you are today, and it may be that we shall become better acquainted.'

The agent spread his wings a little to help him rise to his feet; and he moved towards Cubitt, which was also towards the door, as a signal that the interview was at an end.

'Goodbye,' said Cubitt, brokenly.

The agent held the door open for him.

'Goodbye for the present—Michael,' he said kindly, and he gave Cubitt the least little push between the shoulders.

And Cubitt stepped outside; not on to the fair road from which he had entered the office, but into the rain and darkness of the main thoroughfare of Judge Park.

Now I am afraid I know how the late Mr Dickens would have finished off this story. He would have made Cubitt straightway empty his pockets into the hands of the first tramp, and found some snow to enable him to pelt an errand boy out of sheer good nature. And Cubitt would have raised everybody's wages at the office next morning, and bought the prize turkey for the old charwoman whose oven wasn't big enough to cook it, and invited himself to the junior clerks' Christmas party and made an idiot of himself by dancing there.

But Cubitt did nothing to qualify himself for an asylum, although a change was soon apparent in him. He started giving, and perhaps the agent, hearing of these things, smiled, knowing how desperately it hurt Cubitt to give. And because it hurt him, this was counted in Cubitt's favour. And really I believe the man tried hard to be sorry for those to whom he gave. And that also was counted for grace.

More than that, besides being kind to others, the man began to be kinder to himself. He wore better clothes, and changed his lodgings—to the bitter indignation of his landlady— and sometimes stood himself a bottle of wine with his lunch, and thus gradually became a human being. And these things also were entered on his credit side.

And strangest of all he sought out Gladys again, and found her not only a spinster but extremely unwilling to remain one. She was now a fine woman of forty-one, and looked not a day over thirty-nine, at which age time ceases for all self-respecting women. So he married her; and this again was not counted against him, since he was well old enough to know his own mind. It was on their return from the honeymoon that Cubitt had a queer aberration. They were just getting into a taxicab to drive to their new home, and Cubitt was thinking deeply of something—very likely wondering if fourpence were enough for a tip, or whether he oughtn't to spring sixpence.

'Drive us to Oberon Road, please,' he said.

The man didn't know where it was. But I think he may have taken them there, all the same.

Household Gods

It was nearly a week before we found just the flat we wanted; and at Helmstone-on-Sea, at the height of the season, it is no easy thing to find just the furnished flat you require at the price you wish to pay, if your means are limited. Half the windows overlooked a street of large houses, with a strip of sea visible between the two at the end; but the flat was cheap because the entrance was in a corner of a mews, because half the windows overlooked the cobbled quadrangle, and because of something else which we knew nothing about at the time.

Attwell, Stam, and I were all three bachelors, young, Bohemian, and ex-service men, so that the idea of living over a mews was in no way objectionable to us. Indeed, we desired surroundings a little less prim than are to be found in most parts of Helmstone, whose streets have nearly all an air of solid self-satisfied prosperity.

A young man from the house-agents showed us over. The flat, it seemed, belonged to a Mr Clark who lived in another flat at the opposite end of the mews. Mr Clark, it seemed, was not anxious to let the flat for a short period, but he was willing to accept a low rent for a period of three to six months. The three bedrooms were all of the lodging-house type, but good enough for us, the kitchen was large, unpretentiously furnished, and really comfortable. But a shock awaited us when the house-agent's representative led the way into the sitting-room at the end of the passage. Stam, whose taste was a little severe, peeped in and then collapsed into my arms in a humorous affectation of swooning. Attwell laughed his high staccato laugh and rubbed his eyes. That room was a veritable chamber of horrors.

Fronting us was the fireplace flanked on both sides by low cupboards whose tops formed shelves of the same height as the mantelpiece. Along the mantelpiece and these shelves, stretching from end to end of the room, was an array of vases, glassware and flowerpots that has to be seen to be believed. The predominant colours of these monstrosities were deep blue and gold, but some were light-green, and these carried pictures of hunting scenes and rural villages with very old churches and a few stray cows in the foreground. On the piano on the left of the door there was more of this hideous chinaware, and on a whatnot in a corner reposed two Bo-peep baskets laden with artificial flowers.

'Br-rrr!' shuddered Stam.

'My oculist,' said I to the agent's man, 'wouldn't dream of letting me live in this room unless I wore smoked glasses. No wonder the flat is to let, and going cheap.'

The man laughed.

'They are rather dreadful,' he confessed, if you take the place I should put them all away somewhere. It won't matter to Mr Clark so long as you put them back before you go, and leave the place more or less as you found it.'

The advice seemed sound enough. There was a nightmare firescreen, a stuffed owl, some family photographs, and a few other villainies without which we could live more comfortably. We took the flat for three months on satisfactory terms, and hid the most offensive items on the inventory in the sitting-room cupboards before finally moving in.

On the way before we took possession of our new quarters Stam met Attwell and me on the Esplanade, and announced that he had been round to the flat and had met our landlord as he was coming out of the mews.

'Oh, what's he like?' I asked.

Stam laughed.

'What would he be like? Can't you imagine the kind of man who furnished a flat like that? I should say he's turned fifty, quite well off—that big Daimler we saw there yesterday is his—and probably a retired pawnbroker, or used to keep a pub in the East End. Sometimes a chap like that can be very jolly, but he struck me as being disagreeable. Started asking all sorts of questions about us.'

'Didn't you refer him to the agents who have our references?' I asked.

'Well, we've got to live nearly next door to the man, and I didn't want to seem offensive. I told him you wrote stories, Attwell wrote songs, and I did black-and-white work. He didn't seem frightfully elated at the news.'

'At least,' said Attwell, 'he knows our money's all right, since we're paying in advance.'

'Oh, it isn't quite that. He doesn't like the idea of our running the place on our own, as I told him we should have to do until we can find a suitable housekeeper. He wants everything to be kept just so.'

'I don't see that it matters to him,' Attwell growled, 'so long as we leave things as we find them. If three men who have been in the Army can't look after themselves, nobody can. Did you tell him we were going to take good care of his precious ornaments?'

'I didn't tell him that they were all in the cupboards. Why should I?'

Next day we moved in, and we had hardly settled down in the place an hour when Mr Clark paid us an informal call by casually walking up the stairs and along the passage. On seeing him I made a mental note that it might be as well to keep the downstairs door closed and locked. He found us in the kitchen, arguing as to whether we should sup on cold ham or tongue or go out and dine in a restaurant. He was a big, top-heavy, middle-aged man with very bushy eyebrows and the purplish red face of the heavy drinker. He began pleasantly enough.

'So you're 'ere, are yer?' he said cheerfully. 'Quite comfortable, eh? I thought I'd look in and see that you was orl right, like. My housekeeper, said she was afraid you mightn't be able to manage the gas-stove, so if there's anything you want to know, 'ere I am.'

There undoubtedly he was, and we thanked him cordially enough for coming. We took men as we found them, and because Clark did not know better than to walk unannounced into our kitchen it did not necessarily follow that he was not for all that a good fellow.

'Oh, we can manage all right, thanks very much,' I said. 'Everything's been left very nicely for us to come in, and the gas-stove's perfectly simple.'

'And you won't make too much mess? I know what some of you young fellers are.'

'Oh, that's all right,' said Attwell, betraying a certain shortness of patience. 'We'll look after the place.'

Clark looked admiringly around the kitchen. It was really the most comfortable room in the flat, and, being unpretentiously furnished, it was quite tolerable to an artistic eye.

'Nice little kitchen, this,' he said approvingly. 'But,' he added, with a kind of subdued ecstasy in his voice, 'the parlour's the place!'

Before any of us could think of anything that would stop him he had stalked out of our midst, and was on his way down the passage to inspect the erstwhile Chamber of Horrors. We followed him, rather curious to hear what he would say. He said it within a moment of entering the room.

''Ere!' His tone was loud and indignant. 'What 'ave you done with all them vawses?'

'It's all right,' said I hastily. 'They're in those cupboards.'

'What did you put 'em there for?'

'Well,' said Stam, a little snappily, 'you didn't expect us to live with them, did you? We want a sitting-room, not a public house bar.'

'As a matter of fact,' said I, 'we were rather afraid we might break them, and at least they'll be safer out of the way.'

He stood still and frowning, his face a shade redder.

'They was good enough for my little girl,' he growled.

'Very likely,' said Attwell.

But I had caught what had eluded Attwell, a note of pathos in the man's voice. I felt, if not actually snobbish because the vulgar ornaments had offended me, at least nettled that we should have been betrayed into criticising the taste of this man and his 'little girl'.

'Look 'ere,' he said, with something like a snarl, 'I want them things put back.'

Attwell shook his head.

'I'm sorry, Mr Clark, but it can't be done. You can remove them with pleasure, but we can't have them about the room. It's no use quarrelling over matters of taste. Ours differ from yours, that's all.'

The man rounded upon him.

'I'm not goin' to 'ave my flat turned upside down by you,' he cried.

'Nobody's turning it upside down,' said Attwell, 'and you might bear in mind—will you—that for the space of three months from today, it isn't your flat. When we go we shall leave everything as we found it, and we shall make good any damage we may have done. If you have any complaints to make you must make them to the agents.'

The man was too well endowed with common sense to argue further. He merely swore at us, took a last look round the half-denuded room, and stumped out. From the top of the stairs he called out to us something that sounded like a threat.

'You can do as you blank well please,' he cried; 'but the last parties that 'ad the flat, they shifted the ornaments about, same as you, and they didn't stop long.'

We laughed about him after he had gone, and discussed him several times during the evening. I made a suggestion which amused the others. Referring to it Attwell said, 'Peter seems to think that the flat is full of sacred associations for the man. I don't suppose he's ever lived in it, and anyhow, retired bookmakers—he's one of them for a dollar—don't go in much for sacred associations. Anyhow, if that's his trouble, why does he let the flat? He reeks of money.'

'Perhaps,' said I, half seriously, 'his cupidity has overcome his sentiment.'

'I wonder,' said Stam, 'what he's doing with two flats. No, he must keep this one for letting. I wonder what his little girl's like. There may be a chance for our susceptible Hilary there.'

Hilary Attwell laughed.

'Well,' said he, 'if she's anything like her father I shan't lose my appetite for her dear sake. And did he say that that outrageous room was good enough for her.'

'I believe,' said I, 'that there's a story there somewhere.'

'All right,' said Stam, laughing, 'go and write it, Peter, and take us to Ascot on the proceeds.'

I rose early on our first morning of the flat, wakened by the merry whistling of chauffeurs in the mews below my window, and went into the scullery with the laudable intention of giving the others a cup of tea in bed. There was no matches to hand, so I went into the sitting-room to find some, but recoiled on the threshold from the sight which met my gaze.

The room was just as it was when we first entered it. Each garish ornament was back in its place. The stuffed owl in its glass home looked quizzically down on me from the wall. The coquettishly shaped basket of artificial flowers were back on the dreadful whatnot.

Now in the ordinary way I should only have smiled and supposed that Attwell had replaced the things for a joke. However, I had been the last to go to bed on the previous night, and neither of my friends was of the kind to get up in the night for the purpose of perpetrating such a piece of idiocy. When, later, I told Stam and Attwell, and led them into the room to see for themselves, they accused me, and their surprise eclipsed mine when I denied on oath that I knew anything about it. In turn they too swore an equal ignorance.

We discussed the phenomenon at great length over breakfast.

'One of us,' said Stam, 'must walk in his sleep.'

None of us did, so far as we were aware, if I did,' said Attwell, 'I'd be far more likely to chuck those things out of the window than stick them about the room again.'

'I know,' said I. 'Our pestiferous landlord's got a spare key, and came in last night after we had gone to bed, and set things to his liking once more. I'm sorry we offended the man, but we can't stand that!'

'I believe you're right,' Stam said. 'That's about the only feasible explanation.'

After breakfast we returned the glass and chinaware, and the other offensive decorations to their allotted places in the cupboards.

We then sallied forth to call upon our landlord, certain in our minds that we had him to thank for what had happened, and feeling just sufficiently angry to put our complaint into very plain speech.

I rang the bell at his door at the other end of the mews, and his housekeeper opened it. Mr Clark it seemed was in, and she ran upstairs to call him. Presently he came stamping down to us.

'We want to know,' said Stam, without any greeting, 'what you mean by letting yourself into our flat last night after we were in bed, and replacing all those gimcrack ornaments of yours. Also we want an undertaking from you that this is a piece of impertinence which you won't repeat. I think you had better hand your spare key over to us.'

Clark regarded us all three sullenly for a moment. He did not deny all knowledge of the charge, or laugh at us, as we should have expected him to do so.

'I didn't,' he said, 'and I 'aven't got no spare key, and if I 'ad I wouldn't worry. I don't want to 'ave no truck with you, nor with the flat either until you're out of it. But I warned yer to let them things stay were they were, and I warn yer again.'

'Thank you,' said Stam warmly, 'and now I warn you that if we find you in the flat we shall treat you like a common burglar and hand you over to the police, unless we lose our temper with you and throw you out of the window.'

I expected him to answer violently. He was a big man, and irascible, as we had seen before, but of the four of us he was, strangely enough, by far the coolest.

'You're welcome to,' he answered, 'I told yer I never did it.'

'Then you know who did,' I retorted.

He looked me in the face without embarrassment and answered slowly:

'Oh, yes, I know who did. It was my little girl. I warned yer.'

'Do you mean your daughter?'

'Yes, Mister, my daughter.'

'Then either you had better see that she doesn't repeat the performance or we shall have to prosecute her the next time it occurs.'

He laughed quite mirthlessly but without mockery.

'You might 'ave a job to prosecute 'er. Any 'ow, she isn't under my control anymore.'

'How did she get in?'

Clark shrugged his shoulders.

'Search me! Through the keyhole, I shouldn't wonder. Look 'ere, gents, I don't see why we should quarrel. You've got the flat cheap and you won't 'ave no trouble there so long as you keeps the place tidy and lets those ornaments and oddments be. You've all been in the trenches, and after that a few fall-lalls in a sittin' room shouldn't 'urt you. No need to make a poor girl miserable, is there?'

'I don't see how our arrangement of a room can affect any poor girl who has no right to come into it,' I answered.

'Well, I've warned yer, like I warned the last people. They left in the middle of the night, and the lady spent two months in a nursing home afterwards.'

'Your little girl seems to be rather violent,' Attwell said. 'Well, we've warned you, and any unauthorised person we catch on our premises is going to be prosecuted.'

With that we left him, terribly puzzled by the interview. It seemed that we had to deal with a very obstinate and determined man whose daughter, whom we had yet to see, was as bad as himself.

That night, before retiring, we slipped the bolt on the downstairs outer door, and paid particular attention to the window fastenings. The bolt itself negatived the effect of any spare keys which might be in Clark's possession. Next morning I was awakened by Attwell coming into my room and swearing at me.

'It is you, Peter!' he wound up, before I was thoroughly awake.

'What is?'

'You put all those vases and things back in their places.'

'What, have they been moved back again?'

'They have, and Stam swears it wasn't him.'

I sat up in bed and stared at him. 'Then,' said I, 'one of us is walking in his sleep.'

I jumped up at once and ran along the passage to the sitting-room. It was only too true. The ghastly array of ornaments confronted me as they had done the morning before. I turned and stared at Attwell who had followed me, and we both laughed. There was something uncanny in the business. 'Look here,' said I suddenly, 'have you been cleaning out the room or anything?'

'Me?' Attwell had the right to adopt an indignant tone, as his contribution to the housework was rather negligible. 'Rather not!'

Stam had been listening from his room opposite. His voice reached us across the passage.

'And I haven't got up yet,' he called. 'Why?'

'Only,' said I, 'I was working late last night, and I left behind me a well-filled ash-tray and a grate full of scraps of paper, and it's all gone now.'

Attwell drew a long breath.

'This is getting damn funny,' he said, 'I've been down to the front door and the bolt's still up. The window fastenings are all correct too. It's beaten me.'

We went into Stam's room and sat on the edge of his bed to discuss the mysterious business.

'I think,' said Stam, 'we can acquit ourselves of sleep-walking. Clark admitted that we had to thank his daughter for these attentions. But how the devil does she get in?'

'He suggested the keyhole in his humorous way,' said Attwell, 'and by Jove! I can't think how else she did get in!'

'There's another queer point,' I put in. 'The lady evidently doesn't bear us much good will, so why on earth did she trouble to tidy up the room for us?'

We all laughed. The thing seemed so ludicrous.

'Anyhow,' said Stam, 'I'm not at all obliged to her, and after breakfast we'll call on the agents and lodge a complaint with them. Perhaps that will do some good.'

So intent were we at getting to the bottom of the mystery that we were at the house-agents' office within a minute of the place being opened. The young man who had shown us over the flat was seated behind a desk. Stam, acting as spokesman, began to tell him our trouble.

He interrupted Stam early in his narrative.

'I'm sorry,' he said, 'I advised you to put those ornaments away. There should have been a clause in the agreement to say that the furniture and things wasn't to be moved. The guv'nor told me afterwards; but we were busy at the time and we forgot to have it put in.'

'That doesn't alter our position in the matter at all,' said Stam. 'We should never have signed such an agreement, and besides nothing could excuse these abominable trespasses.'

'No,' the young man agreed, 'he's certainly got no right to come in and shift the things back himself.'

'He denies doing that himself but admits it was his daughter.'

The young man collapsed, bending over the desk in a silent paroxysm of mirth.

'He told you that, did he?' he exclaimed, isn't he a fair knockout? Daughter, eh? He hasn't got a daughter.'

At that moment the house-agent appeared on the scene in person. Seeing us, he asked us into his private room.

'I think I know,' he said, 'what you've come about, and I want to apologise to you. You've been disturbed in that flat you took from me? I am sorry, I ought to have warned you beforehand that nothing was to be moved. The clerk who took you round has not been with me long, and knew nothing about it. Please sit down. I have some cigarettes here if you feel inclined to smoke.'

We sat down, and Stam briefly recounted our complaint. He heard him out, his grey matter-of-fact little eyes gazing dreamily at nothing in particular. 'I am very sorry,' he said again presently, i ought to have warned you. This is not the first time that I have had complaints about that flat. Of course it's true, in a way, that Clark has no daughter. At the same time I can assure you it is not he who comes and disturbs you. It is a very strange affair, it is,' I agreed dryly.

'Now look here,' said the agent confidentially, 'let's see if we can't arrange something. You're very comfortable there, except for that little trouble, aren't you? and you've got the flat cheap. If you'll agree to let those ornaments stop where old Clark wants them to be I'll guarantee you a substantial reduction in the rent you are now paying. Failing that I'll cancel that three months' agreement and find you another place. What do you say?'

Stam answered him with the stubbornness which we all felt.

'After the abominable way in which our privacy has been invaded,' he said, 'we are not prepared to compromise in any way. We shall prosecute anybody we find in the flat, and those ornaments will stay where we have put them. If you had approached us in this reasonable way before we had to come to you and complain it would have been another matter. Today I am going to write to my solicitor about it.'

The agent smiled faintly. Looking back on it all I could forgive him now if he had laughed aloud.

'Your solicitor,' said he, 'will not be able to help you in this matter. You will forgive me for saying that you are all a little foolish. You could all be very comfortable there were it not for this obstinacy, which, of course, I quite understand. I have tried to warn you, and if I have not spoken very plainly it is because I am a business man, and as such I am not going to say anything definite which might provoke your derision. I am sorry, but I can do nothing more but wish you good morning.'

Outside we formed a group on the pavement and discussed this very extraordinary little harangue.

'If Lewis Carroll had invented a house-agent,' Attwell laughed, 'and put him into Alice in Wonderland, I should have expected him to talk like that.'

'I've got an impression,' I said, 'that there's something underneath all this. Everybody seems to be warning us.'

'Rot!' said Stam. 'Clark's a pig-headed man who's annoyed with us for not sharing his tastes, and he's too well-off to care whether he lets the flat or not. He is trying to force us to expose his beastly ornaments and china, and this agent man, for some reason or other, is trying to back him up. We've now found out that Clark was lying when he said he had a daughter.

Therefore he comes into the flat himself and re-arranges his vases. But how he got in and out again last night has me completely beaten.'

'Well,' said I, dropping my voice, 'he can come in and try it on tonight if he likes, and if he goes out through the door on his feet we'll never hold up our heads again. I'll lie awake for the gentleman.'

'That's right,' said Stam. 'Call us the moment you've got him cornered and we'll rush in and join you.'

Attwell chuckled. The prospect of catching Clark red-handed in our sitting-room filled him with a kind of malignant glee.

During that day and in the evening we spoke hardly a word in the flat of what we proposed doing. For all we knew the man had some unguessed-at means of eavesdropping on us. We were careful too to retire at our normal time, so that all the lights in the flat were out at the usual hour.

That night when I retired to my room I only partially undressed. My bedroom was at the head of the stairs, and the sitting-room was at the other end of a long passage, but to reach it Clark would have had to pass my door which I left ajar. I sat up in bed with my ears alert and began a vigil which lasted more than three hours.

In the night silence every little sound in the flat was distinctly audible. I could hear Stam and Attwell snoring in their respective rooms, and smiled to myself at the memory of their saying that they too would probably keep awake. Now and then a board creaked, and something seemed to happen in a cistern overhead, a faint scurrying in the passage outside informed me that we were harbouring rats and mice.

Sometimes my mind would follow a train of thought, and then I would forget to listen until I recollected myself and broke it off. Sometimes the silence would seem fraught with distant and indescribable sound, as if I held a shell against my ear. Sometimes my strained nerves would infest the darkness around me with stealthy motion. It is a nerve-racking business to sit in the dark listening hour after hour.

Just as I was thinking that it must soon be dawn I heard a church clock strike two, and realised that my vigil had lasted only three hours and a few minutes. But it was soon to come abruptly to an end.

The striking of the clock started a new train of thought. I began by telling myself that the night was still young, that it was only one o'clock by the proper time. I reflected then how I had always hated the Daylight Savings Bill, for I preferred early darkness and long evenings even in the summer.

How I hated that extra hour tacked on to the daylight when I was in the army! One went to bed in the light, and rose in it, never seeing cool, clean, memory-laden darkness. About time they repealed the act, now that the war was over. . . .

So far had my thoughts carried me when a sound dropped on my ears and sent scattering everything from my mind but the purpose of my vigil. It was quite a stealthy sound, but unmistakable—the clink of crockery, and it came from the far end of the passage where the sitting-room was.

It was rather a tense moment, although I believed I had nothing worse to face in that room than our very arbitrary landlord. Still, when one has listened long and in vain for a sound, there is always an element of surprise in it when at last it comes. My door was ajar, and as I rose silently and groped for a box of matches, I wondered how Clark had contrived to enter the flat and mount the stairs without my hearing him. Even we, who were getting used to the place, persistently fell over the umbrella stand in the passage, or bumped our heads against the gas-jet in the dark. A feeling of eeriness gripped me, but I shook it off, and having found the matches, slipped out and crept on tiptoes down the passage.

Keeping my head I felt my way round the umbrella stand, and bent my head to avoid the overhanging gas-jet. Then, as I crept up to the sitting-room door, I heard once more the chink of crockeryware from within.

The door stood open. I entered and planted myself a little in advance of the threshold. The Venetian blinds were drawn, and only a very faint light stole into the room between the chinks. This light was just sufficient to show me that I was not alone in the room.

Opposite me was the fireplace, and very dimly I could see that the vases were back upon the mantelshelf. Between me and them something moved, the faintest of faint shadows in the gloom.

I struck a match between my hands, at the same time uttering a loud cry. Then a number of things happened all at once, or so quickly after each other that their action seemed simultaneous to me.

I heard my cry echoed in the bedrooms of my two friends. In little more than a moment they had tumbled out into the passage. Something opposite me in the room made a sudden spring for the door.

I was guarding the small flame between my hands and unprepared for the sudden rush. Someone—something—brushed against me and past me. I thrust out an arm which encountered nothing, and carried sideways by my own impetus, reeled against the open door, which opened further beneath my weight, so that I fell.

'Stop her!' I cried. 'Stop her!'

As I sprang to my feet I listened in vain for sounds of a scuffle in the passage. There were none. I heard Stam's voice crying, 'Hullo, Peter!' and Attwell's shouting 'Anything wrong?' They were on the threshold when I had picked myself up.

'Where's she gone?' I cried.

'Where's who gone?'

'It was a woman,' I said, I swear it was. I didn't see her properly, but she brushed against me. Didn't you see her, you fellows?'

'No,' said Stam decisively. 'Nobody's left this room.'

'She did, I tell you.'

'Well,' said Attwell, 'where did she go then? The passage ends outside the door, and she couldn't have got through the wall. We were in the passage. Are you sure there was anyone there?'

'Quite,' I answered, rather shakily. 'And it was a woman. I could swear that.'

Stam lighted the gas. 'Well,' he said quietly, 'somebody's been here, for all these beastly vases except one are on the mantelshelf, and you will observe, Attwell, that the cupboard door's open, and that one vase is left inside. Peter seems to have interrupted someone whom he thinks was a lady. Peter, you look shaken up. Well, it's safe to assume that she's still somewhere in the flat. All that remains to be done is to find her.'

We hunted high and low, but without result, meeting at last in the scullery.

'I think,' said Stam, 'that a drop of coffee might do us good for want of something better. Matches, Peter?'

'They're in the sitting-room,' said Attwell. 'I'll go and get them.'

We had left the gas on in the sitting-room; indeed, by that time every jet in the flat was burning. Attwell set off down the passage and I watched him from the scullery door. Instead of entering the room he started back from the threshold, swayed, screamed, and fell with a crash. Hurrying to pick him up, and bending over him, I saw through the sitting-room door that the last vase was back on the mantelpiece, but there was nobody there.

We carried Attwell to the kitchen and brought him round by applying cold water.

'This is the last night I'm going to spend in this place,' he gasped. 'She was a girl with frizzed-out fair hair, and she wore a blue dress. She looked at me as if she could kill me.'

Stam and I soothed him between us, and he spent the rest of the night in Stam's room. None of us told the others just then what was in his mind. The occasion did not seem suitable. But we all spoke of seeing Clark in the morning.

We called upon him in a body after breakfast, and as usual Stam did the talking for us.

'Mr Clark,' he said, 'we have come to offer you an apology, and to ask you one or two questions which I think you will admit we have some right to ask. When did your daughter die?'

Clark included us all in one rapid glance.

'Just about two and a 'arf years ago,' he answered. 'You've seen her then?'

'These two gentlemen have.'

'Ah, I was afraid that was going to 'appen. The last people there 'ad the same thing 'appen to them, and all along o' movin' them ornaments. It's no use; my Rosie won't 'ave it! She turned on the wife of the last gentleman who took the place—regular turned on her! '

Attwell shuddered. His experience of last night was fresh in his memory.

'Don't you think you might have told us?' Stam said,

'I did tell yer, but not in so many words. A nice fool you'd have thought I was if I'd said straight out what was going to happen. Besides I don't want it talked of, and I don't want to frighten nobody out o' the flat. Everything would have been orl right if you'd only let them ornaments alone and kep' the place a bit tidy. Tell yer? I'd never 'ave believed a yarn like that if it was told to me, and I didn't expect you to. I used ter think that when dead people was dead they was dead. I've come ter believin' what the parsons tell yer, that there's a place we all go to afterwards, only my little girl, she seems a bit too restless-like to stay there.'

'But what's the reason for it all?' Stam exclaimed. 'Why has—er—your daughter shown herself to us?'

Clark eyed us unemotionally. Whatever he felt he was able to conceal, and he had his voice under perfect control.

'It's like this,' he explained. 'When I retired from bizness about three year ago I took the two flats, the one I'm livin' in now, and yours. My little girl was engaged to a young feller over in France, in the Kenningtons he was. I furnished the flat you're in now as a weddin' present for them, a sort of ready-made 'ome, so that they could get married and settle down straight away. I gave Rosie some cash so as she could buy ornaments and fall-lalls and whatnot, and she bought all them things that you don't like.'

It was then that I lowered my eyes before his gaze, and I think the others did the same. Rather unreasonably, perhaps, I felt ashamed.

'I thought,' he continued, 'that it 'ud be nice to 'ave Rosie livin' near me after she was married, and Rosie fair worshipped that flat. She lived in it, as you might say, and spent all her time arrangin' the ornaments and hangin' the pictures and gettin' her little 'ome just so. After a bit she 'ad a letter from her boy to say that he was cornin' 'ome on leave awmost at once, an' they could get married directly 'e arrived. Rosie got the place ready, even to 'aving salt in the salt-cellars, so as they could marry straight orf and begin their 'ome life there. But 'er boy never came. About ten days after we expected 'im we heard he'd been 'it by a shell as he was goin' down the line on 'is way 'ome on leave. Rosie died about a month later. She wasn't the same girl that she had been, and when the inflooenza took 'er she just went quiet without putting up a fight.'

He paused, but nobody spoke. Sooner or later we should have to tell him how sorry we were, but not one of us could find his voice.

'It seems to me like this,' Clark resumed. 'Rosie still looks on that flat as 'er little 'ome, and it's got to be kept just as she left it. I dunno why. It takes a clever man to understand a girl when she's alive, so who's goin' to understand 'em afterwards? Rosie was my little girl, an' I loved 'er an' thought I knew 'er, but I don't know what's troublin' 'er now. You'd think she'd forget about the old flat now she's found 'er boy again. 'Arf a second, and I'll run upstairs and fetch her photo.'

He left us for a minute during which we stared at each other, and whispered, and made plans for finding new quarters. Then he returned with a large tinted photograph, which he handed to Attwell. I caught a glimpse of a pretty but rather sullen-looking girl with 'frizzed-out' yellow hair.

Attwell glanced at it and handed it on with a shudder. 'Yes,' he said, 'it's a very excellent likeness.'

The House of Unrest

The old chintz-covered settee—almost unfamiliar in its new surroundings—was drawn up in front of the brightly burning drawing-room fire. Eileen made way for me to sit beside her.

It was already half dusk on a winter afternoon, but the room was lit only by the fire. Before my arrival Eileen had evidently been straining her eyes to read by this uncertain light, for a book, half open, lay at her feet.

'Mother went over to Richmond shopping,' she announced. 'I'm expecting her back every minute. Helen's gone to a new school at Surbiton. She'll be back about five. She goes to and fro by tram every day. Cosmo said he'd be home to dinner tonight. I expect he will, as he knows you're coming.'

She shot these pieces of domestic news at me, as it were out of a gun, and added, 'Well, what do you think of the new house?'

Privately I thought it looked a little dismal from the outside. It was one of those double-fronted, detached, stone, basemented houses, which grew up in the suburbs sixty or seventy years ago, and were the fore-runners of the 'compact' modem villa. To my mind there were too many shrubs and trees and not enough space for flowers in the front garden. A semi-circular carriage drive, running between gate and gate and enclosing a sedgment of laurels and other evergreens, gave the place an air of dreary pretentiousness. For the rest, so far as I had seen, one climbed a single step to the front door, on either side of which was a great bow window, one belonging to the dining-room and the other to the drawing-room. The stables were on the right of the house, and on the left was the tradesmen's entrance and a path leading to the back garden.

'I haven't seen it properly yet,' I said defensively in answer to Eileen's question.

'That means you don't think you're going to like it.'

'From the outside,' I admitted, 'I thought it looked a bit damp and depressing. Too many trees and shrubs in the front garden. Still, a winter afternoon is hardly the time to judge a place, is it?'

'Anyhow,' said Eileen, 'we think it's an improvement on that poky little flat. The rooms aren't big, of course, but there's room to breathe in them.'

I looked around in the flickering half light. Eileen's mother's rather solid furniture certainly looked more at home here than in its old surroundings. The Payleys had just shifted their household goods from a block of small mansions in Kensington to this roomier abode at Teddington. They were not too well off. Mrs Payley was Irish, and the widow of a naval officer, who had left her to bring up a family of three. Cosmo, the eldest, an old schoolfellow of mine and a rugger player of repute, was in one of the private banks. Eileen, the second, who was twenty, lived at home and helped and companioned her mother. Helen, the youngest, aged sixteen, was still at school. I—well, I almost counted as one of the family, being a very frequent visitor while I was trying to persuade Eileen to marry me.

'You must come out and see the garden,' Eileen continued presently. 'It's perfectly huge. There's a tennis lawn and a pergola beyond, leading into a great kitchen garden. Mother's in despair about it, because it really needs a man and we can't afford one.'

I laughed; for the Payleys were always refreshingly frank about their poverty. At least twice a month Mrs Payley would assure me, in her rich brogue, that she was tottering on the steps of the workhouse. She would then show me her new furs and introduce me to a huge box of a new kind of liqueur chocolates, which, she would assure me, were the last word in the art of the confectioner.

'I suppose,' I said, 'I'm about your first visitor.'

'No. Noel was round about three afternoons ago.'

'Oh, Noel!' I did not trouble to disguise my tone when I uttered the name. Not that I was willing to admit that he was a rival of mine. He was a mere boy of twenty, and just the sort of youth who would expect to be called Noel. 'One would expect him to come round,' I said, 'before you'd got the house straight.'

'He didn't stay long,' said Eileen. 'He had a fit on the doorstep.'

'A fit!'

'Yes, really. It was dreadful.'

'But what kind of a fit? Epileptic?'

'Yes, I expect it was that.'

I could afford to be sorry for Noel now.

'I never guessed,' I said, 'that there was anything of that sort about him, poor chap.'

'I answered the door to him,' said Eileen. 'He was all right until he'd rung the bell. And then I found him, lying unconscious on the step. Mother and I got him inside. As soon as he was conscious again he wanted to go, and after a bit we let him. It sounds rather unkind of us, doesn't it; but mother and I both thought that he'd be better off at home with his own doctor, who understands him, to look after him. He sent us a line this morning to say that he was all right again. . . . Ah! here's mother.'

We both heard a latch-key in the door, and presently Mrs Payley entered the room like a half gale of wind. She was a tall, stout woman, wearing a blue serge costume and a boa and muff of some sort of black fluffy fur. 'Childhren, childhren,' she cried, 'and hwhy are there no lights? 'Tis straining your eyes ye must be to talk in the firelight. And how are ye, Roger? and hwhat do ye think of our ghrand new family mansion?'

'Roger doesn't like it,' said Eileen. 'He thinks it's depressing.'

'I said nothing of the sort.'

' 'Tis a liver ye have,' said Mrs Payley with her usual frankness. 'A boy of your age should not know hwhat it is to be depressed. Get a move on ye now and help Eileen toast the crumpets; for it's a certainty Alice has let the kitchen fire go black.'

Well, nobody could be depressed very long in the Payleys' company. Five minutes later Eileen and I, armed with two toasting forks, were scorching ourselves over the drawing-room fire, laughing, with our heads close together. I was perfectly happy. Yet, for all that, I did not like their new house. Cosmo arrived home shortly before seven and bore me off to his room to wash, hear the latest anecdote from the Stock Exchange, and listen to what his club intended doing to Blackheath on the coming Saturday.

'What do you think of the house?' he inquired inevitably, as he threw a clean towel at me.

'Ah right,' I said.

'Seems to me a bit dreary,' he remarked. 'Still, beggars mustn't be choosers, and it was pretty cheap as houses go nowadays.'

'Poor old Noel Lampton didn't seem to like it,' I said.

'Eh?'

'Well, didn't he throw a fit on the doorstep on his first visit?'

'Yes, that was very odd. And what's still more odd, he seems to blame us or the house for it. Don't say a word to the others. I found a letter from him at the bank this morning, begging me to get mother and Eileen and Helen out of the house as soon as possible. He said he'd be glad to see us all when we were in town, but he wasn't coming down to Teddington anymore.'

'Silly young ass! If he's subject to fits, he'll get 'em anywhere.'

'Exactly. Not that I'm in love with the place either. Although it's nowhere near anything like a high road, there are tramps about here. I met one in the garden on my way in tonight.'

'Yes?'

'I didn't like the look of the brute, and I had half a mind to ask him what he wanted. But he'd evidently been to the back door and been sent about his business, as he was coming away from there. He came near me and looked up into my face, and it gave me quite a turn—it was so livid and strained and agonized, as if the poor devil were suffering from some frightful complaint. I nearly stopped him and gave him something, but I don't want to encourage these people so they'll come and hang about the house while I'm in town.'

Just then the gong rumbled down below, and two minutes later we went down.

It was towards the end of the meal that Alice, the cook-general, who had been with Mrs Payley for years, tapped timidly at the door and entered.

'If you please, mum,' she said, 'I'm afraid there's somebody walking about in the garden.'

Mrs Payley looked up half angrily.

'Alice,' she said, 'ye haven't the nerves of a kitten. This is tin times in two days ye've heard a man in the garden, and niver a sowl there when we came to look.'

'But I'm sure there's somebody there now, mum,' said Alice, on the verge of tears.

I got up, with a word of apology to Mrs Payley. A young man in love is forever ready to perform even such humble deeds of gallantry as tackling stray tramps.

'We may as well have a look,' I said to Cosmo.

'Right ho, if you like,' said Cosmo, a little wearily. Later I discovered that it was by no means the first time that he had gone in search of a mythical intruder.

At the hall door Cosmo touched my arm.

'You go round to the left,' he said, 'and I'll go round to the right.'

We had our backs to the house, and, facing that way, the stables were on my left. I went quickly thither through the shrubbery path, and found the high gate leading into the yard securely locked. Not content with this, I climbed it and dropped over on to the cobbles beyond. It was while I was peering into the empty stables that I distinctly heard footfalls on the other side of the gate.

'That you, Cosmo?' I called out.

His voice answered me, but from the other side of the house.

'There's somebody here,' I shouted. 'Go round to the front.'

While I spoke I heard the footfalls in full retreat up the path towards the front gate. Then as I climbed the gate of the stable yard I heard them turning the comer around the angle of the house, so that I had no glimpse of the intruder.

I was over the gate in a trice and in the wake of the footfalls. But when I turned the comer of the house I saw Cosmo standing alone in the flag of light flung by the dining-room windows.

'Where is he?' I demanded.

'Yes,' said Cosmo, 'where is he?'

'But I drove him round here not two seconds ago.'

'I know. I heard footsteps. But did you see him?'

'No.'

'I haven't seen him either,' said Cosmo in a queer tone. 'It's not the first time either that I've been out after this same gentleman.'

Well, we beat up the shrubbery and made a thorough search of the garden, but found nothing. Cosmo tugged at my sleeve as we re-entered the house.

'Don't say too much about it,' he begged.

I shook my head, understanding, and we rejoined Mrs Payley, Eileen, and young Helen at the dinner table.

'Nothing there, as usual,' Cosmo grunted. 'As I've said before it's some sound belonging to the house that we can't account for at present. One of these days we shall stumble across quite a simple explanation.'

Helen went to bed before I left, and her mother, after saying good night to her, added, 'And don't forget to say a prayer for the poor souls in Purgatory, Helen.'

The Payleys are Catholics, and it is their common practice to pray for the dead. Yet I might, in the circumstances, be forgiven for reading something ominous into Mrs Payley's adjuration.

I am not often in the City, but I happened to be up next day to see a firm of publishers. In Fleet Street I ran up against young Noel Lampton, who was articled to a firm of lawyers in the Outer Temple. He was one of those pretty boys whom men of a more virile type can hardly help disliking. I didn't dislike him so very much, although he had annoyed me by running after Eileen.

Before he spoke I saw that he was looking pale and washed out. He had lost, for the time being, his pink girlish complexion.

'Been down to see the Payleys at their new place?' was almost his first greeting.

'Yes, have you? Oh, but of course you have. They told me. You've been a bit queer, haven't you?'

'Yes,' he said looking down at the pavement.

'Better now?'

'Yes, thanks. I say!'

'Yes?'

'I daresay you think I'm a fool. I ought to have told the Payleys ... it would be less of a shock. ... Look here, if you think I'm a fool for having fainted. . . .'

'Fainted! I thought you had a fit.'

'I told them that was what it was. I ought to have told them what I'd seen.

Well, you'll see her sooner or later, like I did. And then, if you think I behaved like a kid, go right up to the window as I did, and have a good look at her throat!'

His eyes watered as he spoke, and his voice rose hysterically.

'What are you saying?' I demanded.

'Have a good look at her throat!' he repeated.

'Whose throat? What are you talking about?' I asked.

But he slipped away and was on a passing bus before I could stop him, leaving me transfixed on the pavement, with a hundred unpleasant thoughts chasing each other through my head.

I had promised to take tea with the Payleys again that afternoon—or, rather, I had invited myself. I took an afternoon train down to Teddington, and arrived at about the same time as on the preceding day. It was half dusk, and I remember that the lamplighter kept pace with me about a hundred yards ahead. As I entered the gate I saw a light in the drawing-room, and through the window I could see Eileen and her mother on either side of a cheerful fire.

The other bow window, that of the dining room, was darkened, but the blinds were up; and as I approached the front door I saw something that made my heart jump and set memories of young Noel's words crowding upon me. Out of that section of the bow window that looked straight upon the front door, a face was staring. It was the white face of a servant, for I could see her cap and a pink print dress. I knew it was not Alice, but I began to laugh at the momentary stab of fear.

'Mrs Payley's always been going to have another maid,' I thought, 'and she's got one at last.'

Now a servant looking out of a window ought properly to withdraw herself on the approach of a visitor, but this one did not. As I stood on the step she stared at me with a wild-eyed stare which sent terror billowing upon me in full flood. Her mouth was working, not as if she were speaking, but as if she were shouting or screaming. Never before had I seen a face so yellow and yet so dreadfully mobile. And although she seemed to be crying at the highest pitch of her voice I heard not a sound, nor did her breath cloud the glass in front of her lips.

Now a great fear was on me, that fear which we feel in nightmares, but which is happily strange to our waking hours. I knew that only a thin pane of glass divided me from something which was not of this world and not of God. Yet I could not take my eyes from her, and some force beyond my control compelled me nearer and nearer to the window until our faces were only a few inches apart. And through the galloping panic in my head I heard, as it were, an echo of young Noel's voice: 'Go right up to the window as I did, and have a good look at her throat!'

Already terror had warned me of what I was about to see. But I cannot write in detail of what I saw when the Thing lifted its head. I dare not even think of it. You must guess the rest when I state that the gash had almost severed head from body.

I heard myself utter a loud cry, and that, as in a nightmare, served to break the spell. I withdrew my gaze from that hideous, silently screaming face, and reeled back upon the doorstep. Mrs Payley heard me cry out, and in a few moments the door was open. I caught her hands, and let her draw me into the house as a frightened, half-drowned child is dragged out of a pond.

'Hwaht's the matter?' she cried sharply. 'In God's name, hwhat's the matter?'

I could not speak. Vaguely I was aware of Eileen's white face at the drawing-room door.

'The brandy!' cried Mrs Payley. 'The brandy, child!'

A minute later the taste of raw spirit was in my mouth and I stood staring at them in sickly muddled consciousness. Mrs Payley's strong arm linked itself in mine and led me into the drawing-room.

'Eileen,' said her mother, 'go down to the kitchen and tell Alice to bring up the tea at once.'

I knew, even in the condition of mind I was in, that Mrs Payley had said this to get rid of her daughter, for there was a bell in the room.

'Roger,' she said when we were alone, 'ye've had a bad time, but pull yourself together like the brave boy ye can be, and tell Eileen when she comes back that ye have the heart-weakness. I know just hwhat ye've seen, for Helen's seen her too, and 'twas brain-fever she was like to have. Glory be to God, this is an ill house. But if we put ourselves in God's hands He will let nothing evil harm us.' And she made the sign of the Cross.

'Helen!' I gasped. 'Do you mean to say that Helen saw—her!'

Mrs Payley lowered her voice and spoke rapidly.

'It was after ye'd gone last night, but before we went to bed. We heard a scream up stairs and found Helen lying on the landing. She went to bed early, ye remember. Well, she slipped on her dressing gown and went to Cosmo's room, so as she could get a book and read in bed. And on the landing she met that poor suffering Thing who took her own life or had it taken by another. Eileen doesn't know, but she guesses there's something dreadful about the house. We've had the doctor to Helen. She was near being very ill. She's better now, but still in bed. One av her friends is sitting with her. . . . Some more brandy, Roger?'

I let her give me another tot, and then sat up, clasping my knees.

'You'll have to leave here, Mrs Payley,' I said. 'You must go at once, or you'll all be driven mad.'

'Sure now, 'tis an affair for Holy Church. And who better to deal with it than my own brother at Winter Street? He's told me many stories of ghosts and evil spirits and exorcisms, and, God forgive me, I never believed him! After tea, if you'll be so kind, I'll get ye to go round to the newsagents where there's a telephone and ring him up. Say that he mustn't fail to come down here tonight. 'Tis a matter of life and death.'

I had met Father Donehan, Mrs Payley's brother, once before. He was a Jesuit, a popular preacher, and rector of a fashionable West End Church.

Besides being a priest and a ripe scholar from Stonyhurst and Oxford, he was also a man of the world.

'I'll ring him up with pleasure,' I said.

Eileen came in and we faced each other in some embarrassment. She asked me little about my apparent attack of illness, for which I was grateful. Afterwards she told me that she guessed what was the matter, although at that time she knew none of the details.

I don't know who had the pluck to go into the drawing-room and draw the blinds, but when I went out to telephone, and cast one nervous backward glance over my shoulder, I found them drawn.

Luckily Father Donehan was in when I rang up, but as usual he was full of engagements. I would not tell him why he was wanted so urgently, and I am afraid I needlessly frightened the worthy man by telling him that it was a matter of life and death. But at least I was successful in getting him to come down. Fie arrived by the same train as Cosmo, and the two walked up from the station together.

This was fortunate, since Cosmo was able to tell him the probable reason why his presence was so urgently desired. I could tell by his manner when he entered the house that he already knew a great deal.

Father Donehan was very little like the popular conception of a Jesuit priest. He was tall and of medium build, with a round red face and a plentiful crop of hair just beginning to turn grey. He drank claret with his dinner, and had a whisky and soda afterwards, and all the time he kept up a running fire of jolly conversation that had nothing to do with the eerie reason which had brought him there.

The shock poor young Helen had sustained was one of those ill winds which blow good to someone. She could not be left alone, and the task of sitting with her devolved on Eileen. This left the rest of us free to talk.

'You mustn't think, Mary,' said Father Donehan to his sister, 'that there is anything extraordinary or beyond Nature in these manifestations.'

It was after dinner, and Eileen had gone upstairs to Helen, and the rest of us were sitting around the drawing-room fire.

'I could tell you a hundred such instances,' he continued, 'and though perhaps we cannot help being afraid, we should fear reasoningly and try to pity. If you ask me why Almighty God allows such things, I can only say that I do not know, unless it be to remind us of the needs of the dead. For the spirits who still walk the earth and are visible to mortal eyes are not spirits who have had the blessedness to enter Heaven. Nor are they necessarily lost souls. Perhaps we shall find in time that there is hope even for the most wicked-seeming of God's creatures. Now tonight I will wait up and try to have speech with the spirit of that poor woman, and with that other poor spirit of a man you have heard wandering in the garden. You must pray that I be not too afraid.'

'I'm going to wait up with you, Uncle,' said Cosmo.

'Thank you.' He seemed glad of the offer, i assure you I shall have my full share of human fear, and I shall be glad of your company.'

'And I'll wait up too,' I said.

Mrs Payley tried to deter me, on the ground that I had already endured enough for one day. But I was terribly fascinated at the thought of seeing that woman again, and I felt that in their company I should not be unbearably afraid.

Eileen, who slept in Helen's room, and her mother, both retired to bed shortly after ten o'clock, and left we three men quietly talking over the fire, with the drawing-room door left open. Once we heard footsteps wandering in the garden, but from inside the house there was not a sound.

The hands of the clock were pointing to a quarter to twelve, when Cosmo suddenly gripped my knee. He was staring wide-eyed at the open door leading into the hall, and as I looked awfully in the same direction I saw out of the tail of my eye something vanish around the comer.

Father Donehan was already on his feet and striding towards the door. He must have been suffering an agony of terror, but his gait did not falter. Cosmo and I followed him, jostling at his heels. We heard him catch his breath as if in pain as he entered the hall. But without that, I felt that she was there. I raised my eyes and saw her.

She was standing close against the hall door, with her back to it, facing us. Her head had sunk so that we could not see the horror under her tapering chin. But for the first time I saw all of her—saw the ugly stains on the white apron she wore over her pink print dress. Her face was immobile but infinitely sad, and her eyes burned at us.

Then Father Donehan raised his voice and spoke, and the shock of broken silence loosened my knees.

'In the name of God,' he said, 'who are you? In the name of God, I conjure you to say what you want and what you are doing here.'

She raised her head a little, so that I was afraid, and convulsively closed my eyes. When I opened them again her lips were moving. No sound came from them, but something told me that Father Donehan could understand. It was between these two now. His own lips moved silently in reply.

Perhaps it was for two minutes—it seemed more like hours—this dreadful silent conversation went on between them. Then I heard the priest utter a little sigh.

'Poor child!' he said aloud; and then, 'Take me to him.'

He went right up to her, pulled back the knob of the door and flung it open. In doing so he let in friendly sounds from the world outside. A train was shunting; in one of the houses close at hand a gramophone was playing; in the distance I could hear one of the last trams from Kingston groaning its w ay along to the depot at Fulwell. It seemed so impossible that she should be there. But she passed out silently over the step beside the priest.

I glanced around at Cosmo. He was on his knees and his lips were moving. I knelt down too, and as we crouched, watching, we saw the shadowy figure of a man steal up out of the gloom—the same that Cosmo had seen in the garden on the previous evening. The three formed a group for a moment, and then passed out of sight along the path.

How long Father Donehan was gone I cannot say. It seemed a long time.

We rose up, hearing his steps, and drew free breath at finding he had come back alone.

'They will not trouble you any more, poor souls,' he said gently. He turned and closed the door. 'I have made them a promise,' he added, 'but I fear they will not find peace for a long, long time to come. We must pray for them.'

I never knew what promise he had made them, for he never told us.

Cosmo was first into the drawing-room and I saw him pouring brandy into three tumblers. Then I noticed that Father Donehan's hands were so shaking that he had to use both of them to lift the glass.

'She used to be a housemaid here,' he told us presently in a subdued voice. 'The man was a gardener. They were lovers. In a fit of jealousy he killed her and then himself. It happened twenty years ago. They will not trouble you anymore. They may be here, alas! but you will not see nor hear them.'

And that is the end, or nearly the end.

Cosmo discovered later that such a crime as Father Donehan described had been committed in that house, and we were thus able to discover the names of the wretched man and woman.

Nothing has since been seen or heard of their unhappy spirits, but if you look on the door in the church in Winter Street, you will see, among many black-edged cards, one bearing the legend:

Orate pro animae
MARIAE SMITH
et
JOHANN I BAKER

ad Dominum Deum
nostrum.

The Captain's Watch

Sam Tuckey, who kept the Lugger Inn at St Fay, welcomed Miss Colworth on her arrival and guessed her at once to be a Schoolmarm. And since he never kept guesses to himself— unless they were so slanderous as to be actionable—Miss Colworth was immediately made aware of the impression he had received.

She bridled a little and was able to deny it without contaminating her private well of truth. Nearly a year had gone by since she had relinquished her post at Rosewood School. While proud rather than otherwise of her former calling she disliked the thought of looking as if she followed it.

Well, now she could call herself an artist, lecturer, and—by a trifling anticipation—author. A legacy had come to augment her savings and small private income. It left her free to devote her life to her hobbies, and these were such as were likely to bring more grist to the mill.

At the school she had taught drawing and painting and in her spare time she had produced water-colour sketches which, her friends declared, were almost as good as the work of a professional. Stella Colworth was well aware of her shortcomings, but now that she had leisure she cherished the hope that she was not too old to overcome them. At least she could satisfy an urge and paint to please herself.

Her other interest was folklore, and the twain, now happily united in her, bore her to Cornwall for the honeymoon. For Cornwall has been called Legend Land and St Fay an artist's paradise.

St Fay is built within a hollow of the cliffs and around a harbour-basin. Lime-washed cottages seem to have fallen out of the sky and landed crazily but roofs-uppermost on the precipitous slopes. Stella found the place beautiful in sunlight, lovelier still in the light of the moon, but just a little squalid and depressing in dull and rainy weather.

Since smuggling—once the main industry—had been almost stamped out, the village had known great poverty for close upon a century. The little fishing-fleet—long-liners and seine-netters—which filled the harbour in foul weather, existed wretchedly for eleven months of the year on catches of dog and conger. There was one harvest month when the pilchards came. But when that harvest failed, as occasionally it did, there was tragedy indeed.

Of late years, however, summer visitors had become more frequent. Painters and etchers arrived, and among them some of the famous and wealthy. Other artists brought shoals of pupils who dressed in a manner to scandalise local tastes. Less fortunately 'foreigners' from other parts of England stole a great deal of the new trade by setting up Arte Shoppes and Olde Comishe Tea Roomes.

But the place was still only half spoilt when Stella Colworth first saw it.

Sensibly she avoided the Wee Housie Boarding Establishment and went to the Lugger where Sam Tuckey provided her with an upstairs sitting-room which looked out over the harbour. Stella was delighted—for here was a picture awaiting her brush. She could sit in a plush armchair and paint it when the weather drove her indoors. Out of doors she was confronted with a problem. There was plenty to paint, but there were also plenty to paint it. She found an easel every few yards along the narrow cobbled streets, and she wanted to laugh. It was like something she had once seen in a musical comedy. So this was Legend Land!

Two or three days elapsed before Stella found a pitch for herself, and then her style was cramped by the knowledge that every passer-by looked over her shoulder. But the moment she appeared with her satchel and easel she was on nodding terms with all her brother and sister brushes.

These, when passing to and fro, often asked if they might look, thereby throwing her into agonies of embarrassment and causing her to utter the remark which earned her a nickname. Within a week she was known throughout the village as Only Anne Amateur. But she dreaded the cursory inspections of the professionals. These bewhiskered young ogres were perfectly courteous and made no comment. But after they had passed on she heard muffled laughter, and looking after them saw gestures she was not intended to see. Stella winced and went on painting, grim determination in her eyes and in the set of her lips.

She was on the way to painting something that promised to satisfy her, thus feeding an ambition which required very little sustenance. But so far she had failed in her other objective. She had chatted to many and sundry, but the inhabitants of St Fay simply did not know what folklore was!

Stella was yet to realise that she had been acting like a child naively inviting the confession of an unconvinced murderer. She did not know that these people, who went to chapel on Sundays looking like cockroaches, had secrets and traditions far older than Christianity. She did not know that modem science in the form of radio entered the house of a woman believed by her neighbours to practise witchcraft. Deplorable it was to be ill-wished by her, for only a white witch could remove her spells, and there was none nearer than Plymouth.

In a word there was folklore of a sort before her eyes and all around her, but she was not permitted to see it.

Sam Tuckey, as became an innkeeper, was less taciturn than his neighbours. Besides he had been for many years a sailor in the mercantile marine and his mind had been broadened on the high seas and in foreign ports. But he was loyal to his neighbours—on whose support he had to rely in the dark winter days—and since they chose to keep their secrets from the 'foreign' lady then so would he.

'An old story?' he said, scratching his head. 'Well, there's the one about Farmer Trewinnick's pig.'

It was hardly proper. Boccacio and Chaucer would have seized upon it had it been current in the middle ages. Mr Tuckey, in deference to his listener, bowdlerised it and left it entirely pointless.

'Not quite what you wanted, ma'am?' said Sam presently. 'Ghosts and fairies and witches, eh? Well, folks used to believe in them things once, but they don't today. I did hear tales when I was a boy, but they're all gone out of my head now.'

'Oh, don't tell me you haven't a ghost here!' Stella pleaded, half in fun. She thought that he looked at her rather sharply for a moment.

'Well,' he said simply, 'I was born in this house and I never seen one. And my father before me. And his before him. We're the third generation in this house. All sea-farin' men who settled here in our turn when we gave up the sea. And none of us that I've ever heard tell has ever seen a ghost.' It seemed to her that he stressed that last verb a little, but she affected to take no notice.

'Three generations of sailors!' she said. 'Surely that's very unusual!'

'Oh, we go back further than that. My father's grandfather's grandfather was one of the first men ever to set foot in Australia. He sailed there under Cap'n Cook.'

'Well, that's most interesting!' said Stella, wondering if it were true.

'What's more,' Sam Tuckey proceeded, 'I've got Cap'n Cook's own watch. Or one of his watches. Only it got a speck of sand in it and it's out now, gettin' cleaned up and oiled. I'll show it to 'ee when it comes back.'

'Thank you, I shall love to see it,' said Stella; and wondered if the watch could be classified as folklore in a concrete form.

Upstairs in her sitting-room Stella flattered the unconscious Sam Tuckey by bestowing a great deal of thought on him. If he were much more communicative than his neighbours there was still a substratum of reserve in his make-up. What did he mean by that stressed word when he said that nobody in the house had seen a ghost.

Instinct told her that she was on the track of something at last, although she was not at all sure if that 'something' were the game she had set out to hunt.

Well, if the house did not contain a ghost it certainly contained a parrot, which she was yet to see. Stella heard it imitating the barking of a dog, the mewings of gulls and uttering its own natural cries. She did not like parrots, having once been severely pecked by one, and had not so far expressed any wish to see the bird. She wondered, with a quirk, if old Tuckey would tell her that that too had belonged to the discoverer of Australia!

Stella had already ascertained that Sam Tuckey was a widower and that the woman who kept house and waited on her was his late wife's sister. This Mrs Polrowan, herself a widow, was a hard-featured taciturn woman who rarely extended her conversation beyond 'Yes' and 'No' and i don't know I'm sure'.

She was indeed a dry well for Stella to try to pump, but she must have been in a better humour than usual when she brought the tea that afternoon.

'Yes,' she answered, 'we've a parrot for sure. I dessay you've heard him imitatin' Moreover.'

'Moreover?'

'The dog we used to have. This is a religious household, so we called him after the dog in the Bible. "Moreover the dog came and licked 'is sores." '

Stella hid a smile which she feared would have been damnatory, 'I've often heard the parrot,' she said, 'but I've never seen it yet.'

Mrs Polrowan, already half-way back to the door, turned for a moment.

'Oh, we keep him in our own parlour in the summer when there's foreigners about. If we hang his cage in the bar they comes and teases him. Then they gets bitten and starts creatin'.'

Stella winced reminiscently and laughed. Then as the door closed she continued to smile and sat quite still, looking straight before her, as if hypnotised by a focus of light on the shiny surface of the old brown teapot.

So far she had failed in her quest for folk-tales. But now it seemed to her that she might be on the track of a story of another kind—something more modem, more credible, and even more romantic in its way. It dawned on her that here was rich material for another pen— that, perhaps, of a writer of serial plays for 'Children's Hour'.

Here were the old sailor-turned-innkeeper and his taciturn sister-in-law. Next there was the ghost that was not seen. Then there was the watch, by courtesy and tradition the erstwhile property of the famous Captain Cook. And last came the parrot—an almost inevitable 'trimming' to any tale with a tang of the sea.

She juggled with these four items, turning them this way and that, like pieces of a jig-saw puzzle, but they refused to fit or to form a pattern. Instinct told her that a writer of romances would make something of them, but she found herself quite helpless. As a child her reputation for truth-telling had been acquired only partly by inherent virtue: something at least was due to the lack of an inventive faculty.

The jig-saw pieces remained apart and formless for nearly another week. Meanwhile the student, without being in the least aware of it, had been herself an object of study. Stella's casual-sounding questions had betrayed her to some extent. She was after the stories about the Old People, stories which had been carefully hidden from the compilers of guide-books, stories that had been handed down from the days before recorded history.

Well, Sam knew his neighbours, with whom he had had to live all the year round, and still shared to some extent—without understanding it—their dumb reticence. No man likes to be laughed at for preserving, despite modem enlightenment, a few grains of the strange dark faith of his ancestors. He had travelled to many lands and knew far more of the world than most city magnates; yet if his house were infested by rats he would know that he had been ill-wished. And it was the white witch and not the rat-catcher from whom he would seek assistance.

So if the lady wanted to know how love could be charmed or how the unquiet dead could be made to rest, she would get nothing from him. He would be no traitor to that secret society which bore no name and into which there was no initiation. But if she wanted a strange story she should have his own, and none could deny his right to tell it. She should have it as soon as he was quite sure she would not treat it with derision.

For old Sam Tuckey had taken a fancy to Stella, respecting her for her learning and for being—as his instinct assured him—a 'real lady'. And she should see the watch—which might or might not have belonged to Captain Cook—and the parrot Nero, and hear the tale of the strange link between them. That was—when he was quite sure that she would not laugh at his interpretation of the tale.

Soon after breakfast one morning Stella was on her way out, encumbered as usual by sketching materials, when she found the street door still barred in deference to the licencing laws. Sam came out from the back to assist her. His hand was already on the upper bolt when he paused and said: 'I've got the watch back, ma'am, if you'd care to see it.'

It was dark in the passage and Sam had not the watch in his pocket. At his invitation Stella followed him into a room at the back, a bower of linoleum, horsehair and mahogany. She diverted her gaze quickly from the dingy walls, partly hidden by the spoils of ancient Christmas supplements in gilt frames, to the one small window partly obscured by a large cage and its grey occupant.

The bird stood on its perch, apathetically cracking peanuts, mumbling the kernels and letting them drop almost untasted after the shells. She went over to the cage at once, but Sam, grubbing in a drawer, called out warningly behind her back.

'I shouldn't touch Nero, ma'am.'

'I wasn't going to,' she laughed.

'He's a vicious old rapscallion—even with me. I puts on a pair of old leather gloves when I goes to handle him. They've got him beat, but I feel his beak through them sometimes all the same.'

'Bad, wicked bird!' said Stella reprovingly to Nero. To Sam Tuckey she said: i wonder you keep him if he's as bad as that.'

'Well, ma'am, I've had him ever since I was a boy. I couldn't have been more'n twelve when my old dad brought him home. He must have been a young bird in them days, and what badness he's got in him he must have learned from us. But my dad was fond of him and my dad was the only human creature he was ever fond of.'

'Oh, then, I understand'

'Besides, ma'am, I shouldn't have this old watch if it weren't for Nero.'

He had taken the watch from the drawer and was now holding it up. Stella uttered a faint exclamation of surprise. It was such a gold watch as she had seen only in museums—almost the size of the penny bun of happier days and as thick as a doughnut.

Stella took it in her hands and admired it almost reverently.

'But I don't understand what you just said about Nero,' she said. 'I thought Captain Cook gave it to your ancestor.'

'Oh, don't talk so daft'.' said a shrill feminine voice behind her.

Sam smiled faintly as she started.

'That's my late missus's voice he's copyin'. Gives me a turn sometimes when I forget he's in the room.'

Stella looked aside. Since the late Mrs Tuckey had addressed her husband so often in those terms that the parrot had them by heart it accounted for Mr Tuckey's somewhat chastened air. Also perhaps for his subdued manner to all of the opposite sex.

'About that lovely old watch,' she said, '—I don't see what it could have to do with the parrot. I thought you said Captain Cook'

'That's right enough, ma'am, though I've got nothin' to prove it. 'Tis just the story handed down. You see, my ancestor saved the Captain's life when he was set upon by some o' they cannibals—they got him in the end, you know, ma'am—and out of gratitood the Captain gave him this very watch.'

Stella nodded thoughtfully. Certainly it looked old enough to have such a history.

'It must be very valuable,' she said. 'As a curiosity, too.'

'Oh, I've had all sorts of offers—even from museums—but I reckon 'tis a hairlume. It come down at last to my dad and then from my dad to me. My own boy went under in the war; so when I've done with it it will go to my nevvy. And he'll take Nero along with it if he's got any sense of gratitood.'

Stella was aware of something that she mistook for enlightenment.
'Why, did Nero scream and stop somebody from stealing it?'

'Oh, don't talk so daft'.' said the bird, apathetically dropping a nut-shell.

'It's stranger than that,' Sam Tuckey muttered. 'Maybe you won't believe me, or believe what I believe. But I've made up my mind to tell 'ee, so here goes.

'I was at sea when my old dad was taken sudden with a stroke. I'd done with deep water by then and I was serving on a coaler which hugged the coast all the way down and round from Newcastle. Used to unload from this very harbour and then go on and finish at Penzance. That meant sometimes a night or two at home in the middle of a trip.

'Well, my last trip I never finished. Came home unexpected to find my dad was dying. So I stayed. They shipped another hand who was standin' by here and glad of the job. My dad never recovered consciousness.

'He couldn't move a hand nor speak a word in those last hours, but he was conscious all the time and we could tell by his eyes that there was something important he wanted to say. Mother—she was alive then—and me both knew that it was for our sakes that something was worrying him. So we unlocked his drawer and showed him his bank-book and licence and the will he'd had drawn up all fitty by a lawyer; but his eyes said No.

'After we'd buried him—he had a lovely funeral, and they still talk about the meat-tea we gave—mother wanted me to stay ashore and carry on the house. The licence had been transferred to her by agreement, but the brewers and the licensers both preferred a landlord to a landlady. And although I wasn't married in them days I was glad enough to settle down.

'Well, ma'am, you know how 'tis. Somebody dies and you think the world will never be the same again. Then after a few weeks everything seems to be as it always was. It seems cruel, but 'tis really the mercy of Providence. And maybe we didn't miss the old man quite so much as we might ha' done—because of Nero. Nero had his voice proper, and his laugh. Made us think sometimes he was back in the room with us.'

Sam Tuckey paused to refill and light his pipe, and Stella said: 'Wasn't that rather uncomfortable?'

'Well, you might think so, ma'am, but we liked it. There was something else, though, that we didn't like. I'm comin' to it presently.

'But to get on—it was about a week after the funeral when mother suddenly asked me what I'd done with Cap'n Cook's watch. I'd been meanin' to ask her the same thing. And then it came out that nobody had seen it since he'd been taken ill.

'Well, they're honest folk round here and it never crossed our minds that anybody could have stolen it. We knew too that the old man hid it every night for safety like, but he'd never told us where. And it struck us both at once that this was what had been fettin' him when the time came that he couldn't speak. So we hunted high and low, up and down, everywhere we could think of—but we couldn't find the watch.

'Then one night something happened to give us a shiver. We never covered Nero up until we went to bed, and that night mother and me were sittin' in this room, with Nero just where he is at this moment, when mother says suddenly: "Look at that bird."

'Nero was down from his perch and he'd come to the front of the cage. He was making funny little chirps like he made when he was pleased. And presently he let down his head and began to move it gently up and down, like as if he was being scratched. I've told 'ee my father was the only one he'd let to fondle him. And I'll swear to 'ee we could see the longer feathers on the top of his neck part as if a finger had gone through them. This happened several nights afterwards, and a good many months went by, before the strangest thing of all.'

Stella looked up quickly. Sam Tuckey's words carried conviction. She found herself believing them, and with her curiosity quickened she was unaccountably eager to hear what was to come.

'What was that?' she asked.

'Well, mother and me had been sittin' here quiet as usual, and the bird had been watching somebody that wasn't here. And as usual he'd bent to have his head scratched by nobody we could see, when suddenly he shook out his feathers and looked across at us and spoke.

'I've told 'ee he often spoke in my dad's voice. But this time he said something we'd never heard him say before, and for that matter we never heard him say it again. "It's under the hearthstone," he says in my father's voice—"it's under the hearthstone."

'Mother and me both knew what he meant and what was there. But there's a mort of hearthstones about the house. Howsomever, though, I'd only to slide off my chair and on to my knees to find the right one. 'Tes where I'm pointin' now, and still loose, as I can show 'ee. So I grubbed 'un up with the poker and with my fingers, and underneath I found—but no need to tell 'ee what I found.'

Stella was silent for a few moments. Her gaze roved from the old watch, which Sam had set aside on the table, to the parrot who stood on his perch, now apparently half asleep. He began to wake, however, at the sound of her voice.

'What a strange story! No doubt your father must have taught the bird to say that—in case he died suddenly.'

Sam took his pipe from his mouth and looked absently at the smouldering bowl.

'Oh, 'twas my dad's voice for sure. But there's still one thing we don't know. We don't know whether he taught the bird to say that before he died or—afterwards. '

Stella, conscious of a slight chilliness, had nothing to say. But the silence was suddenly broken by another voice. It proceeded from the cage in the window.

'*Oh, don't talk so daft*' it said.

A.M. Burrage – The Life And Times.

Alfred McLelland Burrage, better known as simply AM Burrage, was born in Hillingdon, Middlesex on July 1st, 1889, to Alfred Sherrington Burrage and Mary E. Burrage. On his Father's side writing already ran in the family's blood as both he and an uncle, Edwin Harcourt Burrage, were writers of the then very popular boys' magazine fiction.

Life in late Victorian times was by no means easy and writing has always been a precarious career for most. For an insight into the young AM and his surroundings it is interesting to see how certain facts were captured in the 1891 census when he was aged one. The family is listed as living at Uxbridge Common in Hillingdon. His father is 40 and his mother 36. In the next census of 1901, and with it the end of the Victorian era, the family has moved to 1 Park Villa, Newbury. In that time his father has aged 17 years his mother 6 years and young AM has disappeared from the records. It's almost a precursor to one of his stories.

There is little documented about his growing up and education. What we can glean though is something about his environment. His neighbours were varied: a tailor's journeyman, a corn porter, a lodging-house keeper and a grocer's assistant. Nothing particularly illustrious, so times cannot have been as rosy as they should, especially in the light of his Father's hard work. Alfred Sherrington wrote for The Boy's World, Our Boys' Paper, The Boys of England,

and various others. He also appears to have written under the pseudonym Philander Jackson and edited The Boys' Standard and that one of his more celebrated pieces was a retelling of the story of Sweeney Todd entitled "The String of Peals; or, Passages from the Life of Sweeney Todd, the Demon Barber".

Sadly Alfred Sherrington Burrage died in 1906. There is a biographical note in Lloyd's Magazine, from 1921, which suggests that young Alfred McLelland was studying at St. Augustine's, the Catholic Foundation School in Ramsgate, and most probably away from home at the time.

A.M. Burrage was 16 years old when he had his first story published; the same year as his father's death, in the prestigious boys' paper, Chums. It was a great start to his professional career and whether doors had been opened by his father and family or not the young man's career now had to stand on its own. He was now primary provider for the household and this was the only way he could do it. His Mother, sister and aunt must be provided for.

Magazine fiction was his family's blood and business and for A. M. Burrage, business was good. He established himself as a competent and creative writer and was busy writing stories and articles on a weekly basis for publications such as Boys' Friend Weekly, Boys' Herald, Comic Life, Vanguard, Dreadnought, Triumph Library Cheer Boys Cheer, and Gem, under the pseudonym 'Cooee'.

However, unlike his father and uncle who had remained firmly and easily categorised as boys' writers, he had his sights set on the more well regarded, more lucrative, adult market. Burrage was aided in his early years as a professional writer by Isobel Thorne of the off-Fleet Street publishing firm Shurey's. Her publications have been characterised as "low in price, modest in payments, but whose readers were avid for romance, thrills, sensation, strong characterisation and neat plotting", and this estimation of her publications also fits nicely the description of Burrage's own writing at that time. For a young writer this sort of readership was vital, and the modest wages he received were bolstered by the exposure the publications brought him. Burrage was certainly helped by Thorne's use of young writers.

At the time Burrage was beginning to really establish himself as a writer, the entire magazine fiction scene was benefiting from what we would now see as disruptive influences: new printing techniques, a growing readership with more disposable income and leisure time and other media failing to provide – though obviously movies and such were only in their infancy at the time. The market was lively and commercial, and the readership interested, excitable and willing to pay. P. G. Wodehouse, of Jeeves fame, recalls these years:

We might get turned down by the Strand, but there was always the hope of landing with Nash's, the Story-teller, the London, the Royal, the Red, the Yellow, Cassell's, the New, the Novel, the Grand, the Pall Mall, and the Windsor, not to mention Blackwood's, Cornhill, Chambers's and probably about a dozen more I've forgotten.

With War clouds darkening the skies of Europe in 1914 Burrage was firmly established as a magazine writer, securing publication in London Magazine and The Storyteller, which were both highly prestigious publications. Alongside he had plenty printed in less illustrious publications such as Short Stories Illustrated.

By now Burrage, a young man of twenty-four-year-was eligible for the Armed Services. Under the 'Derby Scheme' he confirmed that he was available for service if called upon in December 1915. Conscription was to follow shortly though, by that time, Burrage had already voluntarily enrolled in the Artists Rifles.

The significance of Burrage's decision to join the Artists Rifles is made clear by the nature of the unit itself. They formed in the middle of the nineteenth century, a group of volunteer artists comprising musicians, writers, painters and engravers. Minerva and Mars were their patrons, one of wisdom, arts, and defence, the other of war. The unit boasted several significant figures as ex-servicemen, including Dante Gabriel Rossetti, Algernon Charles Swinburne and William Morris. It was a popular unit with students and recent postgraduates, and the training was considered and extensive.

In Burrage's vivid, celebrated account of World War I entitled War is War, he insists that he was a volunteer and not a conscript, though as has already been noted, it is quite possible that his decision to join such a respected territorial unit may have been more of an effort to secure himself a more congenial army posting; had he waited for conscription, he would have had little choice over those with whom he was posted. Unlike poets Wilfred Owen or Edward Thomas, Burrage did not achieve a commission, and he suggests in War is War that this may be a result of his extremely unmilitary personality and his shortcomings as a soldier.

Add to this the fact that as the breadwinner for the family he was putting himself in harm's way. If anything were to happen to him the result on the family would be devastating. With the death of
Edwin Harcourt Burrage in 1916 it came even more starkly into focus.

Even though he was now a soldier he was still a writer and writers had to write. It also helped that it was a distraction from the mindless carnage around him. He experimented with various genres, excelling in the one that was to prove most lucrative for him; the light romance, in which a male character invariably meets a female character, there is a problem or hurdle to their being together, they overcome it and they live happily ever after. Burrage's talent for this formula was such that he could work seemingly endless minor variations from the same basic storyline and so he was able to keep writing a steady body of easy work.

He gives a fascinating account of the practicalities of writing such fiction during wartime in War is War, in which he remarks on the difficulties of censorship: "the problem of censorship was an acute one to me. It was well enough to write a story, but the difficulty was to get it censored. Officers were shy of tackling five thousand words or so, written in indelible pencil..." After some time he managed to find a chaplain who was willing to undertake the censorship. However, in order to secure this chaplain's favour and thus his services he was obliged to appear to be holy. Though he did so in earnest while he was with the chaplain, his efforts were dashed when the chaplain found him, sprawled on top of a young girl, and realised Burrage's piety to be a fraudulent con. As Burrage had anticipated, the reality of his behaviour ensured that this particular opportunity was swiftly ended. Resourceful to the last, though, he writes of his solution: "there were 'green envelopes' which could be sent away sealed and were liable only to censorship at the base, but these were only sparingly issued… I met an A.S.C. lorry driver who had stolen enough green envelopes to last me for the rest of the war; and since he only wanted two francs for them I was free of the censorship from that day forward."

Although we know that Burrage had his family to support at home as an incentive to keep writing, at times in War is War he reveals a more intimate aspect of his relationship with his work.

"It was a great relief to me to write when it was at all possible – to sit down and lose myself in that pleasant old world I used to know and pretend to myself that there never had been a war. Some of my editors seemed of the opinion that we were not suffering from one now. One used to write to me saying "Couldn't you let me have one of your light, charming love stories of country house life by next Thursday." I would get these letters in the trenches during the usual 'morning hate' when my fingers were too numb to hold a pencil, when I was worn out with work and sleeplessness, and when I was extremely doubtful if there ever would be another Thursday".

Writing is a useful therapy and for Burrage it provided a means to escape if only for a short time to a world that he could control and move at will. With the misery and harsh conditions of the War dragging on he was eventually invalided and so he returned to England.

One of the best insights we have as to the character which Burrage presented on his return from the war is to be found in Lloyd's's 1920 publication of Captain Dorry, one of Burrage's story series. In that publication there was included a brief sketch of Burrage, describing his personality.

A.M. BURRAGE is the type of young man who might very well walk out of one of his own stories. He commenced yarn-spinning as a boy of fifteen at St Augustine's, Ramsgate, writing stories of school life to provide himself with pocket-money. Since then he has won his spurs as one of the most popular of magazine writers. Everything he does has charm and reflects his own romantic spirit – for he is incurably romantic and hopelessly lazy. It is his misfortune, although he would not admit it, that his work finds a too ready market. Nevertheless, his friends hope that one day he will wake up and do justice to himself. Otherwise he may end up as a "best-seller", a fate which doubtless he contemplates with equanimity.

Despite the sketch's fairly accurate but negative summation of Burrage's literary output up to that point, some of his stories seem to exhibit a desire to write about more than just his usual romantic plots. The most immediate change of this nature is in his decision to bring some of his wartime experience into his work, despite being perfectly aware that such writing was not at all what his editors desired, for they feared it would upset and intimidate their readership.

An example of this can be found in "A Town of Memories", published in 1919 in Grand Magazine, in which he uses his well rehearsed romantic story with a slight shift of emphasis to explore his own return from the war and the general reception which soldiers received on their return. Following a young officer as he returns to the town in which he grew up, Burrage portrays an almost hostile environment into which he returns; he is unrecognised, and nobody pays any interest, respect or attention to him or his stories of the war, nor even to his reception of the Distinguished Service Order. Instead, the people of the town have their own interests and priorities with which to concern themselves. Though this contentious portrayal of post-war society certainly marks a slight shift in Burrage's writing, he returns to the romantic convention expected of him by reuniting the officer with a beautiful girl who had admired him throughout school.   It would be harsh to not accept that market conditions expected one thing and to ignore them would mean turning his back on publications who still clamoured for his penmanship.

Another of Burrage's alternative directions is to be found in "The Recurring Tragedy", in which a General whose war tactics of attrition had been to the slaughtered cost of his soldiers, and he comes to re-imagine his own past as a Judas figure in a terrible vision. The Strange Career of Captain Dorry became a series for Lloyd's Magazine in 1920 about a gentleman crook and an ex-officer with a Military Cross who, idle in peacetime, meets a mysterious man called Fewgin whose business is in stolen goods and mind reading. Fewgin realises Dorry is a suitable candidate for recruitment into his gang of like-minded ex-military thieves, stealing only from "certain vampires who made money out of the war, and, by keeping up prices, are continuing to make money out of the peace". Again, in this motive, we see a glimpse of Burrage's own feelings on the war, as there is undoubtedly a bitterness towards those profiting from the suffering of others in such a manner. Fewgin justifies himself, saying:

"I help brave men who cannot help themselves. I give them a chance to get back a little of their own from the men who battened and fattened on them, who helped to starve their dependents while they were fighting, who smoked fat cigars in the haunts of their betters, and hoped the war might never end."

Burrage began to see slightly more success in the 1920s, achieving a couple of hard back publications entitled Some Ghost Stories and Poor Dear Esme. The latter, a comedy, concerns a boy who, for various reasons, is forced to disguise himself as a girl. Though these hard cover publications were a notable achievement, and one of which he was proud, the fact was that there was less money in it than in the magazines. In his history of the Strand Magazine, Reginald Pound portrays Burrage around this time, likening him to his equally prolific contemporary Herbert Shaw, considering them "two Bohemian temperaments that suffused and at times confused gifts from which more was expected than come forth. They had a precise knowledge of the popular short story as the product of calculated design. Both privately despised it, though it was their living."

The early 1920s, and with them a boom in prosperity, hope and happiness, now brought with them an increase in demand for war stories. Rather than preferring to ignore the atrocities of the war, which had seemed the general attitude in the immediate post-war years, society became more interested and concerned with the manner in which the war was fought, and the greed and political battles which had necessitated such bloodshed. Burrage answered this demand in 1930 with his own epochal piece, War Is War. He published under the pseudonym 'Ex-Private X', saying "were it otherwise I could not tell the truth about myself", though its publisher, Victor Gollancz, "who published the book and greatly admired it, had to point out that the critics would hardly take the book seriously if it became known that the author earned his living producing two or three slushy love stories a week".

In one of a series of letters he wrote to his contemporary and fellow writer Dorothy Sayers, Burrage bemoans how War is War "promised to be a great success, but was only a moderate one". The book itself was received with reviews on both sides of the spectrum. Cyril Fall's War Books, a survey of post-war writing published in 1930, gives a clear indication as to why the critics were so mixed in reception of the book. He writes:

This book is extremely uneven in quality. The account of the attack at Paschendaele and of conditions at Cambrai after the great German counter-attack are very good indeed; in fact among the best of their kind. But the rest is disfigured by an unreasoned and unpleasant attack on superiors and all troops other than those of the front line, which is all the more astonishing because the author is inclined to harp upon his social position as compared with that of many of the officers with whom he came in contact. He does not use as much bad language as many writers on the War, but his methods of abuse will leave on some of his readers at least a worse impression than the most highly-spiced language.

Dorothy Sayers was the editor at Victor Gollanz for anthologies of ghost and horror stories which included stories by Burrage. She says, in one of her letters of Burrage's story The Waxwork, a piece beyond the nerves of the editors, "what you say about "The Waxwork" sounds very exciting, just the sort of thing I want. Our nerves are stronger than those of the editors of periodicals, and we will publish anything, so long as it does not bring us into conflict with the Home Secretary". Though their correspondence began as strictly business, Burrage's acquaintance with Atherton Fleming, Sayers's husband, allowed their interactions to become less formal and friendlier. Burrage wrote of Fleming "I hope to encounter him soon in one of the Fleet Street tea-shops". 'Tea-shop' being a popular euphemism for the pub, where both Burrage and Fleming could frequently be found, though their alcohol consumption came to damage both their health and their professions, with Burrage coming off the worse.

Happily for Burrage, as a result of being featured in one of Sayers's anthologies, The Waxwork became one of his best-known stories and it would grab the attention of the film companies several times down the years even becoming an episode in the TV series 'Alfred Hitchcock Presents'.

The developing friendship between Burrage and Sayers enabled him to reveal more details of his personal life, admitting to her his "neuritis at both ends (legs and eyes)", and hinting at his troubles with alcohol: "Fleet Street is not a good place for a man who delights in succumbing to temptation, and whose doctor says that even small doses of alcohol are poison to him". Sayers sympathises, replying that Fleming "agrees with you entirely about the temptations of Fleet Street; he has, however, succeeded, through sheer strength of character, in being able to drink soda-water in the face of all his fellow journalists".

In another of Burrage's letters, he apologises for a delay in sending proofs of a story, with the words:

I have had a pretty thin time lately through illness and anxiety. And for days on end haven't had the energy in me to write a letter, and when I had the energy to send a complete set of proofs to you I found I hadn't the postage money (This is when you take out your handkerchief and start sobbing). I owed my late agent over £1000, so I got practically nothing out of War is War. He stuck to it. Well, he is paid off now, and so are my arrears of income tax. All this took a toll of my very small earning capacity, and I have been sold up. This on top of something which promised to be a great success and was only a moderate one, was a bit too much for me. Still, in spite of sickness I am resilient and shall float again. "You can't keep a good man down," as the whale said about Jonah.

For a man who had so many stories in so many magazines, and was gaining pace in Sayers's anthologies as a talented writer of horror stories, his income will have been far higher than the then average wage, and yet as he says, he finds himself short of money.

Several questions are left unanswered about his personal life. It is unclear whether he was still supporting family, or whether he spent the majority of his money on alcohol, or whether he chose to conceal his true fortunes from those around him. Perhaps most incongruous is the apparent absence of a wife; though his death certificate indicates that he had one, listed as H.A. Burrage, he seems never to mention her to Sayers.

He was around forty-two when he wrote that apology letter to Sayers, though in tone and circumstance it seems to be from a man in a far later stage of his life.

Burrage continued writing until his death in 1956, and continued to be prolifically published. Indeed, the Evening News alone published some forty of his stories between 1950-56. His death is recorded at Edgware General Hospital on 18th December, and the causes of his death are recorded as congestive cardiac failure, arteriosclerosis and chronic bronchitis. He was sixty-seven years old, and his last address is listed as 105 Vaughan Road, Harrow.

Though his name is not often remembered in lists of prominent writers of his time, or even it's genres, his ghost stories are highly regarded by critics and fans alike, while his life story tells us much about the trials and stresses placed on authors during and after the war, and on soldiers returning from that war. His reluctant acceptance that the money was in the magazines while the esteem was in the poorly-paying hard covers, and his persistence as a writer, speak of a determined man, doomed to circumstance yet living as best he could.

In ending A.M Burrage wrote a few sentences which best sum up two things. Firstly his love for his son Simon (who sadly passed away in October 2013 and was a great and passionate advocate for his Father's works.) and secondly his succinct reasons for writing.

TO JULIAN SIMON FIELD BURRAGE

who at the moment of writing will
soon achieve the great age of four.
From somebody who loves him.

In War is War I admitted being a professional writer, or in other words one who depends for his bread and cheese and beer on writing, typing or dictating strings of sentences which his masters, the Public, are kind enough to buy and presumably to read.

The book brought me letters from a few old friends and a great many new ones. A large percentage of the new friends, who missed having seen that my identity was rather unkindly betrayed by the Press, wrote and asked (a) who I was and (b) what sort of stories did I write?

The answer to the second question will be found in the following pages. The answer to the first question is 'Nobody Much', worse luck.

Most of these stories were written with the intention of giving the reader a pleasant shudder, in the hope that he will take a lighted candle to bed with him—for candle-makers must be considered in these hard times. Some have already made their bow from the pages of the monthly magazines. The best have, quite naturally, been rejected.